David Ducker is an English carer who now lives in Scotland and cares full-time for his wife, Heather Ann. He is a deacon of his local church and manages the financial affairs of most of the immediate family. He is a father of three with an extended immediate stepfamily.

This book is the life story of Heather Ann – a biographical account of her life. This was dictated by Heather Ann and compiled and collated by her husband, David.

He has previously written *A Time to Laugh, A Time to Cry*.

Heather Ann Ducker

LET ME GET THERE SAFELY

AUSTIN MACAULEY PUBLISHERS®

LONDON * CAMBRIDGE * NEW YORK * SHARJAH

A CIP catalogue record for this title is available from the British Library.

ISBN 9781035822171 (Paperback)
ISBN 9781035822188 (ePub e-book)

www.austinmacauley.com

First Published 2024
Austin Macauley Publishers Ltd®
1 Canada Square
Canary Wharf
London
E14 5AA

Thanks to Brian for helping with the compilation of the manuscript.

Special thanks to Jamie for his tireless proofreading and editing work.

Disclaimer

This is a biography, with names changed to protect the identity of those involved…

Foreword

Hi, I am Heather Ann, the subject of this book. This is my story from my family roots to today. I have written it because I have a message and a point to get across. I would not normally be a person who speaks out or takes centre stage to present or speak, but I have my story, and I believe you need to hear it. It's a story of ordinary life; of my interaction with people who pass me by or rub shoulders with. It's a story of meeting my life partner and the wanderings I endured to find him. The rest you will need to read on. Please do.

Nothing said is intended to harm anyone or to cause offence, and every effort has been made to ensure anonymity, due to the subject matter.

I am very grateful for all those who have assisted me with this project, and all names have been changed to protect identities. First, I want to thank Dave, my husband, who has been a real support to me over these last few years. I have asked him to type up this story of mine from chats and recordings and to add his endorsement and comments at the end.

I am grateful to my family, my children, and extended family and those on Dave's side who are grafted to us as one community, fighting life together with mutual support and most of all love. We have our moments like any family, but I recognise that we are special in many ways with a bond of love that ties us together.

We are grateful to Inverness Baptist Church for their acceptance of us with open arms and pastor Iain for his pastoral care. I could list lots of people who have helped over the years, and I thank you all now; including the ones I have missed or forgotten about. Oh, and thank you, Brian Robertson, who annoyed us both with questions and critiques, but got the job done and also to James for his proofreading skills.

We come into this life with no idea what is in front of us.

We can have influences from all parts: our genes, our family, our social status and social community, our geographical base, our resources, and where we live (even if we are transient), and some would also include "luck."

But some things we cannot anticipate...

I was one of two siblings, but that is part of the story, so I will let you read on...

Chapter 1
Roots

During the Second World War, my mum, Catherine Grant, was stationed in Chatham, Kent, in Great Britain, as a nurse at Chatham Naval Hospital. Although these were tough times, she enjoyed her job and made many friends. She was originally from Embo, a small village near Dornoch in Sutherland in the Highlands of Scotland, which meant she found it difficult at first to make friends, due to her strange accent, according to the Southerners. She had several dalliances with men at the Naval Hospital, where she first met my dad, although I didn't find out who my dad was until I was 16, Reverend Macleod – who was a fighter pilot and a flight lieutenant in the Royal Canadian Air Force. They got on very well for a time, but later, on she caught the eye of a chief petty officer in the Royal Navy, Harry James Backhurst. He pestered and pestered her with gifts of flowers, meals out and dances until she finally gave in and accepted his proposal.

Harry Backhurst and Catherine (my mum) were soon engaged. Catherine had fallen for this smooth talker and found herself with a child, which in those times was a huge thing for an unmarried mother. She had to tell Harry, and this being wartime, things escalated very quickly, and the wedding date was brought forward.

However, a few days before the wedding, Catherine received a handwritten letter from her former flame, Reverend Macleod, pleading with her and begging her not to marry this man, as he would only let her down and cheat on her. He was deeply in love with her, and she should marry him. But he said that, "If you feel that you must marry him, then who am I to tell you not to?" The wedding, however, went ahead, and Rev. Macleod stood back and did nothing more to stop her. So, Catherine Grant of Embo became Mrs Catherine Grant-Backhurst.

After the wedding, things progressed, and mum continued her duties as a staff nurse in the Naval Hospital and Harry continued his role as a chief petty officer on various duties. Mum came back home to Embo on leave, while Harry continued working in Chatham. She received a letter from one of the officers informing her of Harry having an affair with a woman in England. So, she telephoned the naval base asking to speak with Harry and she was told he was on leave with his wife in Scotland. She was furious and told the telephonist that he was definitely not on leave in Scotland with his wife, as she was his wife, and she hadn't seen him for weeks!

My mum had grounds for divorce and her solicitor soon took on the case. A divorce was granted. She gave birth to my brother, Jonas, in Helmsdale Hospital in the Highlands. It was recommended that she stay in Scotland and give up her nursing career down south because of Jonas. This caused much hardship, and she was forced to pick potatoes in the fields with the other local women. Mum also became an unpaid midwife in the village while her mother looked after

Jonas. Harry was ordered to pay maintenance for Jonas. Mum spent several years working hard and on occasion spent happier times with a lady we called Auntie Ina in Brentwood in Essex. Other short breaks in Felixstowe were taken with my Auntie Janet.

On several occasions, Mum went down south to spend time with my dad, Reverend Macleod, who had been corresponding with her all along, especially after he heard that his suspicions about my stepfather were correct. He didn't delight in the fact that he was right about Harry but offered a shoulder to cry on and before long they became close. Mum fell head over heels in love with him. One thing led to another, and mum became pregnant with me. My dad was on active service in England and Canada, so couldn't spend much time with her.

Mum was living in a house in Embo which my grandfather Alexander had built with his own hands. She lived there with Jonas while carrying me. It was a happy time, so I've been told; with everybody rallying around helping where they could, a real community atmosphere.

Mum wrote to my dad telling him I was due to come into the world soon and he was incredibly happy and looking forward to coming home and settling down with his sweetheart, as they had planned to marry.

But he never made it home. Sadly, he died on military duty, leaving mum without her man and me without a dad. Mum didn't know what to do and began to weep a never-ending supply of tears for the man she had loved and who loved her so dearly. To this day, we still don't know exactly what happened to him, nobody seems to want to talk about it.

Mum was afraid of what might happen to her as unmarried mothers were still frowned upon. Mum had thoughts of giving me up for adoption, but the rest of the family said, "No! She was put on this Earth for a reason." My grandmother decided to send mum and Jonas away on holiday to Felixstowe with Auntie Janet, whereupon I made my appearance in this world!

It was on the morning of Wednesday, 24 May 1961, just after midnight when mum told my Auntie Janet, it was time, and an ambulance was called to transport them to Ipswich General Hospital, where at approximately 2.30 a.m., I was born.

Obviously, I don't remember much about that day, but here I was and am to stay, Heather Ann Grant.

Mum decided to stay down south for a few weeks to recover. This holiday turned out to be anything, but I've been told that although the weather was great and rest and relaxation was the order of the day, mum grew increasingly restless and was getting homesick. So, after my first few weeks of being born an English girl, we set off just over 600 miles north up to mum's home.

Embo is a small picturesque former fishing village nestled on the east coast of Sutherland in the Highlands of Scotland. It had a small population of about 200 people and here I was making it 201! Embo is home to Grannie's Heilan' Hame—a holiday resort.

My memory of it is a few streets with cottages, a sloping road down to a harbour similar to that of Helmsdale or Brora, a deep stone harbour with rope ladders with wooden steps hanging down the square blocks of harbour walls where you can see the tide marks with the changing colour of moss and wet weeds. As I think of this, I am sure I can smell the seaweed at King Street and Front Street. Then I'm reminded of the Post Office which supplied most of the retail needs of the village. 'Grannies' has a fish and chip shop near the caravan site. There are a few shops selling fishing nets and stripy wind breakers and all matter of holiday items.

All you need is the Sun.

Hiring of horses was a nice pastime and the fares were used to pay the handlers. I loved to see the joy on their faces when they went off to the shore for the day. I would like to see some day the horses back and doing their trips along the sand.

Of course, any sign of fishing is down to a few hobbyists and the sound of girls gathering to gut the fish at the side of the harbour is long gone. Strangely enough, there is a link to the southeast.

The nearest town of mention is Dornoch just a few miles south of the village. It is known primarily for two things: golf and the cathedral. Yes, Dornoch has a cathedral, so according to old traditions, that would make it a city!

Dornoch town is populated with a good percentage of retired people and has a castle and a few shops to cater for both the routine supplies and the whims of tourists.

Embo, being smaller, has little to it apart from the rows and rows of small cottages that seem to hug the coastline, not dissimilar to the Moray coast where Local Hero was filmed more years ago than I care to remember. I suppose, as the crow flies or the fishing boats of years gone by sail, Dornoch and the coast of Sutherland is relatively near Banff Buchan and those lovely fishing villages along the sea front to Fraserburgh.

I was born a cute baby with short blonde ringlets with a rosy, chubby face. What's not to love? At first, we went to see my grandmother, who was overly excited to see me. I was presented to her in my Silver Cross Pram—all chrome and leather with removable carrycot. What a proper cutie I must have looked in a wee frilly dress with a bonnet. As it was such a small fishing village community, all comings and goings were an important thing, and everyone came out to see this new arrival.

As I grew through my first three years, mum was a homemaker for us, my brother Jonas and me. Jonas was a wee terror, or so I was told. He was a mischievous little boy and into everything. It makes sense that I should follow suit. At three years of age, after my terrible twos, I was taken to nursery in Embo. It was attached to Embo Primary School. Mum got a job at Grannies Heilan Hame working for Jim Mackintosh, a kindly gentleman who took pity on my mother. She was a waitress and bar manager at the popular holiday site, which exists to this day and is still a thriving business.

Sadly, my grandmother Esther passed away.

As we went to my gran's house, she had been laid in a coffin in the sitting room and I was asking questions about where my gran was. But someone told me she was sleeping in the box on the table. I ran over to her without anyone noticing at first and began trying to shake her awake and telling her to get up as it was me. People were horrified when they saw me, and I was dragged away kicking and screaming not knowing what I had done wrong. My mum led me away and said my grandmother was at rest, in peace. But I guess I still didn't really understand.

At four years old, I went up into big school-proper primary school. This was a substantial change for me, but I quickly made a lifelong friend Eleanor. We became best friends. My mum also knew her mum and dad when they lived on a local farm. Life was becoming a wee bit better. Eleanor's dad also worked in the local slaughterhouse; her mum was a particularly good friend of my mum's. Several times a month, my mum would get a knock at the door in the early hours of the morning when John Gordon, the local funeral director asked for her help to dress the dead and as I was only wee and couldn't be left alone, I had to go with her. The worst time was my first time going with her. There was an old man who had passed away while on the toilet, and I needed the toilet, and they told me not to go but I darted straight in and just screamed and stood there frozen to the spot with fear. I was led away by a lady while my mum and the undertaker worked to remove the elderly gentleman from his position. After my first brush with the dead, however, it soon became a regular thing to go with my mum but this time, I stayed where I was told to, still scared of what I saw. I had nightmares for years. However, things never turn out the way we plan them. Mum was corresponding with her old school friend who was also a nurse during the war who had moved to Felixstowe, and she became restless once more.

This friend was a lady called Winnie and she was telling my mum about all the opportunities in the seaside resort in England and mum decided to rent out her house in Embo and move south again to Felixstowe in Suffolk, England when I was about seven.

Jonas, my brother, had signed up to the British Army in the 4th Royal Tank Regiment. He left for his basic training just as we left for England.

Mum got us a flat to live in and she was helping a lady who ran a travelling fair which was based in Felixstowe. I can't remember the name of the fair, but I remember the lady: as I said, she was called Winnie. She was a medium build brunette, and I was fascinated with her fashion sense—she wore skirts and stockings—much more modern fare than the traditional dresses worn in Embo. She was a lovely lady, very bonny and friendly, but she had major problems with her husband who was an alcoholic, and she was grateful to my mum for her help. We went to view a flat and were told that the previous tenant, a lady had recently committed suicide in the flat by putting her head in the oven. The landlady hoped this wouldn't put us off. It surprisingly didn't and we were very happy there.

Felixstowe is a seaside port in Suffolk which has been suitable for short crossing to France. The population there is over 25 thousand people; so you can imagine the difference to our paltry 201 in Embo. I had not appreciated till lately that the Southeast Coast of England and the Moray Coast of Scotland are linked by the sea and seafarers. During the days of herring fishing, there were often boats, with the registered initials of their home port, in harbour, from so far away that you would not expect to see them. The fishermen would follow the fish around the coast and in some cases their wives and girlfriends would travel ahead to prepare to work at the gutting of the catch. "Not my kind of job," I hear you say.

Also, I heard of mission workers from Suffolk and Norfolk who would travel with the fishermen and when the fishermen were ashore, they would hear the preaching of these men.

A famous Scotsman from Moray, Jock Troup did this preaching and was heard as far south as Suffolk and as far north as Wick!

While we lived in Felixstowe, I went to Causton Junior School on Maidstone Road in Felixstowe. I absolutely enjoyed my time here and was getting on quite well. Mum was annoyed by my school and went to see my teacher as she didn't trust me. She accused me of throwing my homework away, but my teacher said that they don't give out homework as the children needed to rest their brains.

I was enjoying myself so much so that I got on an electronics course; I was really coming on and my teachers were full of praise for my efforts. But as they say all good things must end.

Mum received a telephone call from her friends in Embo telling her to come home, as her house had been wrecked and vandalised by the couple who had rented it. Not only that, but they had stopped sending her money for the rent. So, we were headed north back to Embo to live for good, which quite annoyed me, but what could I do. Mum knew best.

The couple who had been renting mum's house in Embo were very apologetic about the lack of rent money and promised to pay it all back when they returned home to England. They also said that they needed to return home to be closer to family. The house was in such a state and had to be totally redecorated, which all fell to my mum to pay for, as the couple never got back to her about the missing rent.

At the tender age of 12, I was to attend Dornoch Primary School. This school and its atmosphere were quite different from my former English school, and it was very nerve-wracking. The lessons were different and more mental arithmetic and not as advanced as in England. Also, we had tons of homework up here and the pupils were not at all kind. I was being picked on daily and teased about being English. They were calling me a Sassenach, a derogatory term for a foreigner. I made a friend in another English child, his name was Keith, and we became good friends and looked out for each other against the bullies. There were also two girls who were nice and kind to me, they were Lorna and Penny, whose father was the postmaster in the Dornoch Post Office. I was also reacquainted with my old friend Eleanor; she was so delighted that I had moved back to Scotland. She also introduced me to her cousin Amanda; we were all particularly good friends and still are to this very day.

Life began improving. By that I mean I began to change from a very shy young girl, who wouldn't say BOO to a goose, into an outgoing young lady unafraid of anything. Mum got a new job in the Co-Op, living in the flat above the shop. It was lovely—with plenty of rooms and more than enough space for mum and me. Every time I came home from school, I used to help mum out in the shop with shelf stacking and cleaning.

I stayed in Dornoch Primary School until the age of 13. I then moved up into the academy next door to the primary school. It was here where my life began to change completely. One cloudy dull day, I went to the academy and the day was going on normally when a young lad called Gerald about the same age as me, started calling me Sassenach over and over in the playground. I thought about what my mum had said to me a few days before that she was not going to fight my battles, I had to stand up for myself. He attacked me, and I flew into a rage and tore his jumper to shreds. The crowd were egging us on to fight more but Gerald stopped and left in floods of tears yelling at me, "I'm going to tell my mum."

I just smiled and said, "Go ahead then. I'm not bothered." When I arrived home, mum asked me if I had a wonderful day in school and as I was a wee bit flushed, and she wanted to know what had happened. So, I told her of the bullying, and she seemed proud of me. A short while later, the doorbell went, it was Gerald and his mum. She was shouting at me and my mum for ruining his jumper. But mum told her what had happened, and his mum was furious with him too. She made us shake hands and apologise to each other and to stop this nonsense! There were no further incidents.

One day my PE teacher was shopping in the Co-Op where my mum worked, and she had a quiet word about me. She told my mum that I was getting very lazy and suggested that she take me to see the GP to see if anything was wrong with me as I was always complaining about being very tired. Mum took me to see our GP Dr John Macleod, but he just said that there was nothing wrong with me, I was a very lazy girl. Mum was disappointed by this and said that I was having extraordinarily strong chest pains, which he shrugged off as being just ordinary growing pains without even examining me and said that I would be fine.

Chapter 2
Growing Pains

Things continued as normal until at the age of 14, I developed severe pains in my belly and I was rushed into the Lawson Hospital in Golspie, in an emergency ambulance. There they found out that I had acute appendicitis and needed an operation to remove my appendix. The year was 1973, and it was Christmas Eve, it was a mild day with snow on the ground. Before they could operate, the anaesthetist was checking me over with my blood pressure and heart tracing, when he became genuinely concerned and asked to speak to a specialist heart consultant. The consultant was telephoned and offered to come from Wick to supervise the procedure as I later found out that I had a heart murmur. It took what seemed an age for the consultant to arrive and the operation progressed after a final check over by him.

Post-op, I was told I would have to attend Raigmore Hospital in Inverness, to see a heart specialist about this murmur. They prescribed tablets for my condition, and he spoke with me and my mum saying that I had a major problem with my heart and due to this heart murmur, I couldn't get an operation to help me, but the pills will be the best option for me. Also, I would never be able to have children in my life as

I could die or have severe complications giving birth. So, I went home with my mum all upset and confused as to why I would never have a family. Mum said that maybe it was for the best. I hated those pills. They were very big and tasted horrible.

A few months later, it was summertime, I went swimming with my cousins in the North Sea off Dornoch Beach. Swimming was and still is my favourite thing to do. It was a lovely warm summer's day, and my cousins Sandra and Samantha wanted the three of us to make a bet to see who could swim out the furthest. There was a boat anchored a way out in the sea and this was decided to be the target. We were all excited and started out to swim towards the boat. We swam for what seemed ages and my cousins quickly gave up and returned to the shore, but as for me, I thought I could do it and with my stubborn streak continued towards the boat. I almost made it, just a few yards more and I would make it. But then I got severe chest pains and had severe cramp. I started shouting for help, but I began to panic and sink. I must have swallowed a lot of sea water until I eventually passed out. I don't know anything about what happened next or how I was rescued until I was told later.

I awoke coughing up salt water and this strange man was giving me mouth to mouth. My top of my bikini was missing and there was a large crowd around me. I heard people talking saying how it was disgusting and tutting. He wrapped me in a foil blanket and carried me over to his nearby caravan. I was shivering and in shock and he sent my cousins to fetch the doctor and to find my mum. The doctor arrived first and checked me over. Then mum arrived in shock and panic. The doctor said to me, "She is incredibly lucky to be alive. What a silly thing to try and do." The stranger had saved my life and was thanked and congratulated by both the doctor and my mum. My cousins looked terribly upset and concerned for me. Mum hugged me and gave me a stern look and a telling off before thanking the man who had saved me. He told my mum that he was an off-duty police officer from England who was on holiday in Dornoch with his family. Mum said to him that she would get him a drink that night at the marquee dance for the Miss Highland show queen competition.

The evening approached and at the showground in Dornoch, near the airfield, was a huge marquee surrounded by caravans with lots of people milling around all waiting around for the dancing to begin. It was the Highland Agricultural Show dance. We arrived in my pretty little dress and saw the gentleman who had saved me before and mum bought him a drink as promised and he checked to see if I was ok.

HEATHER ANN BACKHURST (Miss Embo)

A wonderful time was being enjoyed by everyone, when the compere announced that the guest star, Welsh actress Nerys Hughes, who was to be the judge in the show queen competition was arriving soon, and we were to get ready. The excitement began to build and in the crowd of about 1000 there were 12 contestants all wanting the title of show queen. At 14, I was the youngest. The time came for the competition and as we all lined up on the stage, we were all introduced to Nerys Hughes, and we were all excited because we knew her from television on playing the part of Sandra Hutchinson in the 'Liver Birds.' I discovered she was as lovely as she was on screen.

She was stunned to see me as 'Miss Embo' especially as I was only 14. But I was still allowed to enter the competition. It was Miss Dornoch who won the competition, I was a wee bit upset but was asked back to Nerys Hughes' caravan to receive a special gift from her.

She presented me with a necklace of the Old Man of Hoy, while her husband looked on smiling. It came time for me to leave and Nerys' husband, Patrick offered to escort me back to the tent, but I said that I would be fine.

So, off I skipped out of the caravan. As I neared the tent, I was grabbed from behind and a man tried to get on top of me and ripped my knickers off yelling something in a Wicker accent. I tried to scream but he had his hand over my mouth. I managed to wriggle, and I screamed and kicked him, and he ran off. I rushed to the tent where I found my two cousins Sandra and Samantha, my eyes filled with tears, and I cried and ran off towards the beach where I sat on the pier staring into the water wondering what to do. I couldn't see for the stinging water in my eyes and my cousins eventually caught up with me and asked me what happened, and I just said I wanted to die. They managed to coax me to go back towards the marquee where we found a policeman to whom we told the story.

My cousins were sent to find my mum. As they neared the marquee, my mum had just come out to see where I was. They were out of breath and mum asked them what had happened, and the girls said that a Wicker man had just tried to rape me around the back of the tent, also they said how they had found me on the pier thinking about taking my own life because I felt so dirty.

But I was scared of what she might say and was very shaken when she appeared at the door of the police caravan, shocked and concerned. She just hugged me and told me I was safe, and it wasn't my fault that this had happened. The police brought me a white overall and asked me to remove my clothing and put the overall on.

The police were conducting an extensive search of the grounds and marquee but couldn't find him. I was taken in a police car to the police station and was met by a policewoman and examined by a doctor. The doctor said I was just shocked and traumatised by this dreadful experience and I should go home and rest. I was only bruised, and my mum was relieved that I had not been badly hurt. I had to show the police where it had happened and then I was allowed home. But just before they let me go home, I got a talking to from the police as well as my cousins. We were never to go to big dances on our own or even to the toilets alone or go anywhere alone as it was not safe. My mum said she would make sure of that. To my knowledge, the police never did find the man but at least I had survived this ordeal.

The next day was a Sunday and I started to get back to normal again. I had a lovely day with Samantha and Sandra and my mum. We were discussing what had happened on the night before and mum explained what the police meant, and we just enjoyed each other's company trying to forget the previous night's events. We shared a lovely meal together in the house until their mum arrived to pick them up to take them back home to Alness. I went to have a shower and got my school clothes ready for the next day and mum tidied up before going to bed.

On the Monday morning, I awoke and got dressed ready for breakfast when my friend Eleanor came down to the house to see if I was ready to go to school. She asked if I had a wonderful time meeting the Liver Bird Nerys Hughes? I said yes, I enjoyed it very much. I showed her the gift which I got for being the youngest girl. It was a necklace with a figure of the Old Man of Hoy engraved on a stone on the necklace. I loved it and treasured it.

Eleanor said, "You are very lucky to get to meet Nerys Hughes!"

I said, "Yes, I was very lucky."

But, if only she knew the rest, which I kept from her.

Eleanor had a big mouth and could spread it about. I didn't want people to hear what had happened at all and certainly not second hand through Eleanor. I wouldn't want that as I felt dirty enough.

So, we just had a good day at school and didn't tell her anything else. At lunch time, I decided to go and see my mum as she was working in the Co-Op, I took her aside and said to her not to say anything about what happened the other night to me.

She said, "Of course not, it's bad enough it happened. I will not say a word. Just be safe, Heather Ann, and remember you can't have any boyfriends because of your heart and if you ever fell pregnant, it could mean death for you and the baby."

I said to my mum, "What little faith you have in me. I will keep myself to myself. But what happens when I leave school then?"

She said, "You will have to protect yourself then." I then went to have my lunch and afterwards Eleanor and I decided to walk back to school. We went to our English class and all the children were fooling around and my teacher said, "Can you all be quiet, because if not you will be up here at the front of class, and I will belt each one of you!"

We were told to do our essay and during the essay, a boy and a girl behind me began playing with my hair and throwing paper about while the teacher was writing, and I got annoyed and told them both to stop it. They continued and I just threw the paper back when the teacher lifted her head and caught me doing this. She shouted at me to come up to the front of class where she asked me why I was throwing paper around. I told her what happened, and she got the others up with me. She got us all to face the front of the class and she got the belt out of the drawer.

She told us that this is what you are getting from me, but your parents will get the report from me of what happened today. Also, you will get heavy homework to do as well, and it must be returned finished by tomorrow morning.

We were all very frightened. She 'whacked' us twice on the hands. It wasn't pleasant.

I got home first and managed to do the heavy homework. Mum came home and I had to have a wash and help my mum with the dinner. I said to her that I had had a dreadful day at school. To which she replied, "I know because I received the report from your teacher. That was not right and very naughty."

I looked down glumly and agreed. The night continued with not very much else said. I gave her a hug and went to bed.

Next day, I got up and made mum a cup of tea and toast and got ready for school. I went on a slow walk with Eleanor to school and met up with Amanda and a few others, chatting about what we were going to be doing that day. Just after we arrived at the school yard, the bell rang and we all got into lines and headed off into assembly where the head teacher gave a short talk, and we sang Amazing Grace. Then after a wee prayer, we were sent to our classrooms to continue with our day. Everything seemed to be going well and it was very enjoyable until I was told to go to music class, and I was told to play the violin, but I didn't want to play it as my friends had told me that it can cause a double chin when you get older! I told the teacher it wasn't for me, and could I get another instrument to play which I would enjoy. I decided in my own self to get a guitar to play. I enjoyed this very much and I was doing so well, I showed my music teacher who was extremely impressed. She said can you play it. I said yes, then she wanted me to play in front of the class. Everyone was amazed and some were very jealous.

I left my guitar in the classroom when we went on a break and soon it was time to go home. I picked up my guitar in its case and headed home, thinking everything was fine. I put the case in my room and didn't think about getting it out until I had to practice some songs, when I eventually got it out of the case, I noticed that someone had cut the strings. I was very upset about this as I had been told I was good at it. To this day I never found out who had done this dreadful thing to me.

At least the rest of our days were good; we spent many happy hours out with the girls, Eleanor, Amanda, Penny and Lorna but we had to wait until our homework was done first. Penny and Lorna's dad was the postmaster in Dornoch Post Office. He was a lovely guy, always cracking jokes with the customers, ensuring they always left with a smile to carry on with their day. On the weekends, I really enjoyed helping my mum with her job in the Co-Op stacking shelves and cleaning the floors. The customers always smiled and told my mum how proud she must be of me helping her out. When I had done all the work mum asked of me, I would take the shopping home and light the coal fire to make it warm for mum returning home after a long shift. The kettle was on ready for a nice cuppa after each workday. I never shied away from work, and it gave me a purpose and covered the need to be wanted or accepted.

Mum was always happy for me to help. She said, "One day when you get older, you will be as delighted as me when someone does the same and helps you."

I giggled and said, "Really?"

"Yes," she smiled, "Really!"

As days went by, things started to get a bit better, the routine of time of school, home, sleep etc. That was my life while in Dornoch Academy.

At 15 I graduated to Golspie High School. We all had to get the bus there as it was quite a long way from Dornoch.

In the highlands, bus trips to school were the norm and in fact, some pupils would stay over in the town because of the distance or because they lived in remote places or even on the islands.

The bus was run by John Gordon, who was also the undertaker who Mum was working with dressing the dead. He always made sure we got to school on time and safely and back home again. Mum said not to take any nonsense from other more disruptive kids on the bus with us. She even gave Eleanor and me a good talking to that morning before she headed off for work. So, we went on our own little way on the bus to our new school, laughing and joking with Amanda, Penny and Lorna and all the other new students.

Golspie, with a population of less than two thousand, is in Sutherland and is located North of Dornoch. It's a pleasant run up the coast. It was the seat of the Countess of Sutherland and the famous castle close by is Dunrobin Castle. The thing that one sees from the north or south of the town on the approach is the Ben at Ben Braggie, the tall mountain to the west. It's a hill walker 'must do,' probably on their 'Bucket list.'

On the top of the Ben is the 'Mannie,' a statue of the First Duke of Sutherland. A controversial monument to the landowner responsible for the most notorious of the Highland Clearances. That's a subject that was never taught when I went to school.

As we arrived at the school, all seemed very strange and huge, nothing like our old school in Dornoch. The culture and outlook seemed more grown up. It was also strange going to different classes, in different rooms, and meeting lots of new people. Some would say we were quite overwhelmed by it all.

We soon got used to our surroundings and were enjoying our new classes until we got to the art class. Things took quite a sinister turn.

Our art teacher was a young man and although I can't remember his name, I still remember him, and he was quite handsome and very kind and sweet for a teacher. He was however extremely interested in my friend Eleanor and her work. Some of the girls started to tease Eleanor that this teacher fancied her. But she kept insisting that he was much older than her and she wasn't at all interested saying he's not my type and they all started laughing. The bell rang for us to clear up our work and go to the next class, but the teacher asked Eleanor to stay behind to finish off her art drawing. Everyone else had left to go their classes and when I arrived at the next class, the teacher did a head count and said that we're missing one pupil. We all looked at each other and said that it was Eleanor and that she had been asked to remain in the art room to finish her work.

The teacher looked puzzled, and she asked me if I could go and fetch Eleanor from the art classroom as she shouldn't have stayed behind. She would be having words with the art teacher after school. "Of course, Miss," I said as I walked quickly away to the art room. It wasn't long before I got to the art class and the room was empty. I knocked on the door, but still with no reply.

I opened the door and walked in. I saw the storeroom door was slightly open and I heard voices inside. I peeped inside the open door and saw him doing bad things to Eleanor. I was shocked and upset. But I gathered my thoughts and knocked loudly on the door. Eleanor sorted her clothing, and the teacher did also. The art teacher said, "Good work, Eleanor.

well done, off you go to your next class." So, I walked quickly with Eleanor who was very red in the face. I said what were you doing in there? She said nothing and I said that I saw something bad through the door. But still she stayed silent. Her face said it all. All the other kids were sitting in the classroom laughing at Eleanor's red face and saying what were you doing in the art classroom? She said tidying up the mess which everyone left behind. But the teacher looked less than convinced or impressed at the reply.

The day continued and next was cookery class. Our teacher had decided that we should make a Christmas cake and we were all to bring something from home to go in our Christmas cake. So, we took a note of what was needed. As the time came for us to go home, we went on the bus. A coach with disabled children was driving behind us and Amanda noticed it she told Eleanor, and they were both pulling faces from the back of our bus. Eleanor was being horrible to them making nasty sounds and calling them terrible names. I got upset and told her to stop doing that or one day you'll get a disabled child of your own and you wouldn't like it. She laughed at me and swore at me. "No f'ing chance of that." So, she carried on taking the mick out of them, thinking it was funny.

When we got back to Dornoch, I bid my friends farewell and headed home. My mum was home, and she asked if I had a good day at school. I told her everything that went on in the art class and during the day, and Eleanor taking the mick out of the disabled kids. She said, "Oh my goodness," which is not good. She said, "Heather Ann, I hope you weren't doing anything like that as God doesn't like disabled kids being mocked and it might come back on you." I told her that I hadn't, but I was trying to stop Eleanor doing it. But she wouldn't listen. I then said about our cookery teacher Miss Fagg had said we need some stuff to put in our Christmas cake. So, mum gave me some stuff, but not the stuff I was after. But I didn't mind. We had dinner and I washed up and went to bed.

The next day was another school day, but everyone was quiet and nothing much happened. However, on the way home, there was a group of lads saying to us if we wanted anything we could always ask them and they would get it for us even cigarettes, drink anything at all. So, I said can you get me some brandy for my Christmas cake as I would love to surprise my mother with a good Christmas cake, and they said they would love to do that for you Heather just bring the money for it and we will get it for you. I said thank you to them and carried on heading towards the bus stop. These lads were from Golspie, and we all waved to them from the bus as we headed home.

When I got home the house was empty and I went to check where mum was and found out that she was working late. So, I lit a fire and made us some dinner so that when mum arrived home, she would have a hot meal ready on a plate. When she finally returned home, she was so tired but very happy that I had made some dinner for her. She said, "Thank you, Heather Ann, for that lovely dinner you made for me."

I was very happy that evening. Mum and I watched some TV and afterwards, she was talking about the good times she had had in her nursing career and the lovely friends she had made during the war. She told me how she had met Harry Backhurst and then how she had met my dad and the events surrounding their relationship and the wedding. But she didn't want to talk too much about my dad as tears began to well up in her eyes, so she cut it short, and we went off to our beds. Now, at this time we had a white Alsatian dog called 'Sheba,' she was a lovely dog and everyone in Dornoch knew her and loved her. She was my ever-present companion when I was at home, and she often came with me to my bed. Tonight, was no exception as she followed me to my room and as I climbed into bed she jumped up and came for a cuddle as usual then settled at the foot of the bed. I knew I would be safe whenever she was around.

The next day, I got up ready for school, waved to mum and Sheba as I left the house with my pocket money which I had saved. When the bus arrived at Golspie, I spoke to one of the boys who we had met the day before and asked him to get me a bottle of brandy so I could put it in my cake. They asked me for the money and said they couldn't get a large bottle with the money, but it will be a half bottle. I said that would be ok. So, they left and said they would see us later. As we went on our lunch break, sure enough, there were the boys with my half bottle of brandy. I thanked them and put the bottle in my bag.

After lunch was cookery. We all got the ingredients ready for the cake and started to mix it together. I put a bit of brandy in the mix, and we let them cook for a wee while, while we cleaned the kitchen. After a few hours and a separate lesson in Maths, we went back to the cookery block where we all got our cakes out of the ovens and let them cool. My teacher said we had all done very well and especially me as my cake smelt wonderful and that my mum will be so proud of me as it was excellent. She also laughed and said, "She will also be very tipsy."

I also giggled and replied, "Yes, but at least she will sleep better."

"Yes, she really will," was her response.

I put it into a sealed tin and poured the rest of the brandy in the cake. It smelt strong, but I knew mum would love it. I left my cake in the school with the rest of them with our names on each tin and waited until it was time for the icing.

Things were moving faster and faster, edging up to our last Christmas together at school and we all began asking each other what we were going to be doing after we leave school. One said they wanted to be a prison warden, she was from Hamilton and her name was Alison, who was a lovely girl always dressed as a tom boy. Amanda and Eleanor didn't say much about what they wanted to do, but as for me, I wanted to go into the Forces and do nursing just like my mum had done before. We all had our own ideas and dreams of how our futures might happen. But nobody knew just how it would happen after leaving school.

So, everything was going well at school. Eleanor kept her dark secret about the art teacher as she didn't want anyone to know about it as he was much older than her and they would take the mick out of her. Plus, her father would destroy him. Also, it was her word against his. And who would they believe a young schoolgirl with teenage crushes or a grown man who was in a position of authority, her teacher no less. So, I had to keep my mouth shut and not say a word about what happened, and I wasn't very happy about holding the secret.

When I got home from school, I had a chat with my mum. She said, "Is there something bothering you, Heather Ann? I can see that you are worried about something."

I said, "Can you keep a promise?"

She replied kindly, "Of course, I can."

"I have to tell you something serious that happened a while ago and it's been bothering me."

"What is it child, spit it out! It can't be all that bad?" I said that when we were in the art class that day when she was teasing the disabled kids, something happened.

"Well, child, tell me, I promise I won't be cross."

"The teacher was a very nice young man, but much older than us. We were all doing our artwork and when the bell rang, we were told to pack up our stuff apart from Eleanor. She was asked to stay behind with the teacher. We all went to our next class and that teacher asked me where was Eleanor? I was asked to go and get her as this was not on. I did as I was told and when I got to the classroom, there was nobody in the classroom. So, I went into the room and the cupboard door was slightly open and I could see through the crack in the door that he had his trousers down and Eleanor was slightly undressed, and I was shocked. I stepped back and knocked on the door. The teacher said, 'That's fine, Eleanor, off you go now.' If I hadn't got there in time, they would have been having sex. Oh, Mum, it was awful, and she told me not to say anything."

Mum looked shocked and calmly said, "If there had been another person there with you, you could have reported it. But as it was only you, he could say you were a liar and Eleanor would be scared too. It would be your word against his. So, I suggest that you don't say a word about it until it happens again and next time take someone with you, so you will have a witness. Then he would be called to see the Head Principal."

So, that was the end of that, and she said she would keep it to herself. Funnily enough though, we never saw or heard of the Art teacher after that day. Maybe he got found out. Who knows?

The very next day, it was time to ice our Christmas cakes. So, we iced them all lovely with soft white peaks and a soft royal icing with Happy Christmas stuck on the top. I was so proud of myself, and my teacher said so we should be proud of ourselves and our achievement. So, I put my Christmas cake in the tin I had brought from home, and we headed home on the bus all feeling chuffed that we had done a great job on our Christmas cakes.

As I opened the door, mum said, "What's in the tin box?"

But I just said, "It is a big surprise for you that I have made in school, and I hope that you like it."

She blushed and said, "I can't wait until I see it. It will soon be Christmas, then you can open the box."

She was pleased that I had made something at school, and she could see that I was proud to bring it home. She asked me to help her make dinner and then we could have a chat about our days. I said that there wasn't much to say, as school was winding down for the Christmas holidays. So, we left it like that. We made a lovely, tasty dinner and we both watched the news as mum always liked to keep up with what was going on in the world. I went to wash up the dishes. When I returned, we chatted about how school had been that day, not mentioning the icing and decorations on my cake as it was a surprise. I just said that everything was going well, the classes were ok and even the bus journey every day was fine. We were all getting excited with the approaching Christmas holidays. I had a wash and put on my pyjamas and bid mum goodnight and went to bed to read a book. As I was a teenager, I loved reading romance novels, filling my head with the perfect man of my dreams and thinking of how my life would be when I got married.

Some days were better than others, but we plodded on and got our work done. Until one day, it all went a bit wrong. That day, we were due to have a gym class, I loved doing gym and exercises and always looked forward to it. We were split into girls versus boys at football representing our hometowns and rivalry was intense. Everything was going well at first, but I couldn't run as fast as everyone else.

I started to get severe shortness of breath and pains in my chest, feeling very tired and sickly. I had to be helped off the pitch and told to rest in the classroom until it calmed down. The gym teacher said, "Why are you having trouble like this all the time? You're a young lassie and should be out there enjoying yourself."

I said, "I don't know, Miss. I just wish I was better and able to run about like everyone else."

She told me that she would have to write a report about this to the head and to your mother. I said that I knew that.

"I will have to report about you being breathless with pains in your chest."

"I'm sorry, Miss, for being a pain," I said.

"Don't you be worrying now," she said. "We'll have to get this looked into."

After the gym class was over, the class all came back into the classroom, all chatty and laughing when they saw me on my own with the gym teacher. They were not very nice to me and called me a chicken for not playing football with them. But when I tried to explain about the shortness of breath and sharp pains in my chest and arms, they just said, "Are you sure you aren't just lazy and want to sit down and rest and become the teacher's pet?"

This really upset me. I wasn't lazy or telling lies and tears began welling up in my eyes. I yelled if they knew what I'm going through all the time, they wouldn't be going to school at all, and would just stay at home pleading not to go in. I told them all to shut up. So, they all just sloped off to their seats in a mood and said nothing more. But the looks on their faces said it all. If looks could kill, I would have been dead long ago. The other classes went by just fine, we just got on with our work until it was time to go home.

I was so glad to get home on the bus. What a day! When I arrived home, I chatted to mum about what had happened at the gym. She sighed. "Heather, what can we do? Get your heart checked again? But I don't think they will be able to do anything for you here. You're a young girl and when you leave school, things will change for you for the better. It won't be long until you leave school, then the world is your oyster. But until then you'll just have to do what you can."

I helped her with dinner and washing up and went to bed with everything we had talked about buzzing around in my head. *What should I do? What could I do especially with this heart problem? Whether I join the Forces or work in a shop, or work in a factory, I will make a life for myself and see the world!*

All night long, I slept with dreams floating around in my head.

As I awoke, I felt excited and rushed downstairs for breakfast. I made breakfast and set the fire for my mum. She asked, "How are you feeling after yesterday?"

41

I told her that I was fine and had decided to join the Forces when I had left school. Then I can go places and see more of life. She was pleased and said, "Good for you. But they will have to give you a medical and see if you're fit enough to join up." I said that I understood but they may just pass it. Mum just nodded a knowing nod. She must have thought I was just being stubborn and whatever she said I would take no notice anyway. I got ready for the last day at school before the holidays, we were all so excited, and it was Christmas time. We all went on the bus, filled with excited chatter, to school. Everyone was hoping for a good Christmas with lots of presents and food. We had Science, English and Art and everything went very well, until the time came for us to say farewell to our classmates, which was very sad. We wished everyone well, hoping they would all have a Happy Christmas and a nice New Year, and we would see each other next year. As we neared home on the bus, it all became quite teary as we waved off our friends until it was my turn to get off, then we cried and wished each other well.

I walked through the door and started tidying up for when mum came home and lit a fire, then started to make some dinner. I put the Christmas tree up and decorated it. Mum came through and asked if I had a good day. I said that it was all good today and we had all wished each other well and wished everyone a very Happy Christmas and a good New Year but it all was a wee bit sad as well. Mum said that was a nice thing to do. She turned to me and asked me what was in the tin that I had brought home from school, as it was very heavy, and she was wondering what it could be. I had told her she couldn't open it and she stayed true to her word and hadn't even had a peek. I told Mum, "As it's nearly Christmas, you

42

can open the box if you must! You can see my surprise for us and see if you like it." Mum went and fetched the box and put it on the table and her face said it all, as she lifted the lid very gently. She was like a wee child opening her first ever present. "Wow!" She smiled as the warm smell of brandy filled the room. Her face was a picture and it lit up the room. "You did all this yourself? Well done, you. I'm so proud of you, my girl." I just said it was amazing what I can do on my own, without anyone telling me different.

Mum was so proud of me and my Christmas cake, that when she saw Sheena the postie, she gave her a piece to try, and she said she loved it. Sheena asked me what on Earth had I put into the cake as it's so lovely? I just laughed and asked, "Why do you want to know?"

"It's just fantastic," she said.

I told her that seeing as it was the last Christmas at school, I wanted to make a special effort and put brandy in the cake. Several people had some of my cake: my brother Jonas, his fiancée Leslie, Sheena the postie and her friend Sharon. They were all amazed and asked me to make them one. I laughed and said, "It'll cost you!"

They laughed too but I said, "I'm serious," with a smirk.

Christmas came and a good time was had by all. It was lovely having turkey with all the trimmings and Christmas pudding too. The house was all aglow with the fire smouldering and everyone was full of food. I was so full that I thought I might burst.

Chapter 3
Hopes for the Future

After the New Year celebrations were over, mum and I sat down for a serious talk about the future. I was definite that I wanted to find a job away from home. Mum looked concerned and said, "Do you really want to leave home?"

"Yes, I really do. I'm nearly 16 anyway and I'm going into the Forces anyway. I would like to try the Army or the Navy or even the Air Force. I would love to train to do nursing in one of them, anything to take me away from this place. Not you, Mum," I said as she wiped a tear from her eye.

"It's just Dornoch and the people in it. I can't be like them drinking all the time, I want a career!"

She agreed and said, "I wish you all the best for that," as we weren't sure if my heart would let me down.

Jonas came down for a while over the holidays and he said, "Why do you want to go in the Forces?"

I said, "It is a good life and a good wage."

He said, "Heather Ann, yes it is a good life, but it's a hard life. If you pass the medical, we'll all be overjoyed."

Everything was going well, and schools and colleges were going back for another term. I decided to go back for a few months until I was 16. The head teacher tried to put me off leaving early saying that I needed to do my exams, but if I was determined then he couldn't stop me and he wished me the best of luck in my future life. I finished the week and on the last day I gave a present to my favourite teacher, Mrs Smith. I said, "It was nice knowing you. Thank you being a good teacher, but things must change for me. I am leaving school to get on with my life and see the world." She agreed with me and wished me all the very best in my future life and career, whatever I choose.

We didn't do much else apart from watch a movie and we also had to write down what we wanted to do with our lives when we left school. I told my teacher what I had always wanted to do, join the Forces as a nurse and see the world. She was amazed and asked me if I would manage the IQ test? (Cheek!) I thought as I laughed it off. "But the rest of the test I'm sure you will manage just fine." She smiled. So, we had a chat about my future and what it entails. She told me there would always be a place for me here if I couldn't manage the test. "Thank you," I said with tears in my eyes.

The days continued it was the same old lessons, Maths, English, Music, Science, History, Geography, Biology, Art, and Cookery. It was the same every day until I left school.

When it came time for me to leave school, I tearfully bid them all goodbye. They replied, "If there is ever a problem, remember, we are always here for you." Soon it was time for the bus to take us home, my last journey from Golspie High School was a very tearful one, but I was determined to do this. I had a chat with Eleanor and Amanda, they said I was mad leaving school so early. Why couldn't I wait that bit longer and all of us leave together? I told them that I just needed to get on with my life. I can't just hang about with you guys and drag my heels. They weren't happy about it.

I got a part-time job in The Fountains of Dornoch making bracelets and rings and all sorts. Mr Fountain asked me if I would like to go full time until I get into the Forces. I jumped at the chance as I was really enjoying the work. Little did I know that he was a retired captain in the army. He asked me which of the Forces I was considering joining. I told him that I wasn't bothered which of the Forces I went for as they would all give me a good career. My mother had had a good career as a nurse in the Royal Navy during the war. He told me that the IQ test was a wee bit hard, but the medical was a great deal harder. He said, "My dear girl, I wish you all the luck in the world." So, I listened to him as he was the more experienced.

On one of my days off, I went with my mum to the Forces careers office in Inverness. On pay day, as we always did, we caught the bus from Dornoch for our planned shopping in Inverness to treat ourselves. I went into the Careers Office ahead of mum and I thought that I would try the Navy first.

I went to the Navy desk and the gentleman was very nice to me and asked me how he could help me. I told him that I was interested in a nursing career in the Royal Navy just like my mum did during the war. He nodded to my mum and said he was pleased to meet a veteran like himself.

He said to me, "You will be there for up to two hours max and your dear mum can do her own thing and come back later. If you haven't finished, she can wait for you in the waiting area."

I was so excited thinking that this was my future about to start. I was led through the double doors where I was given a pen and some paper, and I was told to sit down at a desk where another paper was upside down. This is your first test. It's an IQ test. "Off you go," he said.

I turned the paper over and just stared at the sheet with funny writing and symbols on it. I just put my head down and got on with it. It was very hard, and I had great difficulty doing it. I was not allowed any help with the test. I felt that I had managed very well with it.

After I had finished, I put my hand up and the gentleman walked over to me and took my completed sheets and escorted me to another room for my medical. I had to remove my clothing for the female doctor to check me over. They checked my breathing, my heart, my height, my weight, my eyesight, and my pulse. They didn't say much and told me to put my clothing back on and wait in the captain's office. I was very nervous and tried to calm myself down before I got to meet him.

The captain came into his office with the papers from both the test and the medical and sat down at his desk. He was a lovely gentleman, very tall and thin, smart with his Navy uniform on and very kind and well spoken.

He looked me straight in the eyes and said, "How much do you want to be in the Navy?"

I answered him and said that I would give my life to be in the Royal Navy as a nurse or a sailor. He said, "Do you want to follow anyone who has been in the Navy?"

I answered, "Well, yes and no." He asked me what I meant by Yes and No? I answered him that I wanted to see more of this life and the world, and the only way was to join up. Plus, my mum was in the Royal Navy during the war as a nurse in Chatham Royal Naval Hospital. I think that she would be so proud of me following in her footsteps. I continued, "It's in my blood to carry on the family nursing tradition."

He looked at me and smiled. "Good girl. You would make a fine nurse. You did well with your IQ test but sadly you failed on your medical."

With tears welling up in my eyes I asked him, "What did I fail on?"

He put his head down and said, "Your heartbeat was abnormal and if this was fixed you can return to us, and we would gladly take you on. I'm sorry, but that's just it. We can't accept you like this."

I broke down in tears in front of him and he put his arms around my shoulders, and he said, "I'm so sorry this has happened as you seem so keen to join the Royal Navy."

He gave me a tissue and led me into the waiting area where my mum was waiting for me. Mum asked me how I got on. The captain just looked at her with a frown and spoke

"She is very upset, madam. She passed her IQ test but failed the medical."

It was a definite no. She asked, "Why what was wrong?"

He said, "It's her heart, I'm afraid to say. Until she gets the problem sorted out, we can't take her on. But as soon as it's sorted out, we would have no hesitation in taking your daughter on."

Mum gave me a big hug and said, "Oh dear, not so good. Never mind, Heather Ann, there will be something out there for you, you'll see."

I said sniffling, "Yes, nursing! But I can't get in."

She replied, "You will, sweetheart. Trust me."

We boarded the bus and went back to our home in Dornoch.

At dinner time, mum opened her bag and said, "I got this for you as a treat."

She handed me a bottle of expensive perfume together with a silver necklace with a silver cross on it. It was lovely. I was welling up with tears as I said, "Thank you."

Mum said, "You should wear the cross and keep Jesus in your heart and one day in the future, he will advise you where you should go. Your heart problem will be sorted my child and you will be able to thank both Jesus and the surgeon for it."

So, I put the cross on and smiled a weak smile and said, "Mum, you shouldn't have done this for me. It's too much."

She smiled a beaming smile, saying, "Darling, you are my favourite child. Why can't I do this for you? You always help me, and this is a small way of saying how much I appreciate what you are doing for me and for being with me."

I was now in floods of tears after hearing that she thought so much of me, even with all my heart problems. My brother Jonas was never there to lend a hand. He always wanted to be with Leslie. They were never there, and everything always fell to me to help. This formed a deeper bond with mum, more than ever before and my love for her grew stronger. I think she felt sorry for me with my heart problems and doctors fobbing me off with pills all the time and saying that I'm not allowed to ever have a family ever. But I persevered and took it all in my stride. I had to carry on and live my life as best I could for now. I decided to carry on with my job at Fountains of Dornoch until I had decided what to do next.

One day, Eleanor and I decided to have a wee walk along the beach. It was summertime soon and there were caravans and tents full of holidaymakers as far as the eye could see. We decided to stop at a bench facing the beach and began to discuss our future. What would we do when we left home and when could we see ourselves doing it? Eleanor was unsure about leaving home as all her friends were there and she would miss all the fun times they have together. These were her confidants and drinking buddies. I was not into drinking at that age or into partying, but she was heavily into it. She said that she would get terribly homesick and would never be able to stay away from home for long. But she would always try to come and visit any of us that did leave.

As we were chatting, two young lads came over and asked if we would mind them joining us. Eleanor said to them, "We don't mind do we, Heather?" I didn't know where to look and my face was flushed. I was terribly shy, and mum had always said we should never talk to strangers. Eleanor was chatting away in good style while I just stared out to sea. She asked them whether they were there on holiday and where were they from. The boys said together, "Aye we are, we're from Glasgow." I still stared out to sea and felt a lump in my throat. They asked us whether we were on holiday too? We laughed together and said, "No silly, we're locals!"

They smiled and said, "That's nice. Could you show us about the place, and the pubs?" We agreed and they asked our names, and we asked them theirs. The boy with dark black hair said, "I'm Jacques, and this is Alex."

"Pleased to meet you!" We replied in a chirpy tone. Eleanor introduced us both to them. Jacques' arms were full of tattoos, and he had a denim waistcoat on. He looked a real hard nut. Alex was blonde with only one tattoo. They turned out to be nice lads, hard on the outside but caring on the inside.

When we got talking to each other, Alex was sliding over towards Eleanor. I was quite a bit shy, and Jacques was the same although didn't want to appear shy with his hard man look. He moved closer to me, and we shared a smile. Before long it was time for me and Eleanor to return home for our dinner. We asked, "Could we see you both again tomorrow?"

They looked a wee bit down and said, "Can we see you both later instead?"

"Make a time and arrange a place to meet and we'll meet you there," we replied, grinning wildly. So, we looked at each other with excited eyes and agreed on the meeting place. We arranged to meet right where we were sat as it was easier.

"How is 7 to 7:30?" This was to give us time to have our dinner and clean up afterward, and time to walk down to the beach. The boys smiled and said, "It's a date!" We all smiled and said goodbye to each other.

When I got home, the smell of mum's cooking filled the house and it smelled lovely. She asked what I had done all day and where I had gone?

I said, "We went for a walk to the beach to chat about our future, but Eleanor's not for leaving home as she'll get too homesick and miss all of her friends."

"Aww, that's a shame."

I said something also happened at the beach seats. She lifted her head and looked me in the eyes saying "Well? What happened?"

I mentioned about the two lads who had come over and asked to sit with us. I explained that we got chatting. They were here on holiday from Glasgow. Mum gave me a stern look and said, "Heather Ann, you shouldn't be chatting to strangers. You just don't know who is out there. There's lots of perverts hanging around and you both need to keep safe."

I said, "We are safe, Mum. They're decent guys and very polite too. We've made a date with them, as they want to get to know us. We decided together to see them again and we'll never be apart."

Mum said, "Be warned, anything happens to you, or your heart and I will never forgive myself for letting you go. But promise me that you'll stay together and not separate."

I promised mum that I would be very careful.

The time flew by, and it soon became time to meet the guys. We skipped arm in arm to meet the boys, grinning from ear to ear. Lo and behold there they were right where we had left them. We greeted each other and began chatting again. We had a good laugh chasing each other on the beach, and everything was perfect. We were getting along so well; we almost forgot the time. We could hear the clock chiming and we decided it was best for us both to head home. We apologised to the boys and said, "It's time for us to go home. Our parents will be worried and come looking for us if we're not home soon." Jacques and Alex said they couldn't remember when they had last had such a good time. They asked if we could see each other again. I said it would have to be late afternoon, as I was working. They were very interested and asked me what I worked as. I just said, "I make jewellery for now but am deciding to leave to go for a nursing career." So, we set a date for the next day. Jacques and Alex both gave us a kiss on the cheek, before we parted. We both blushed and ran home, giggling all the way.

As we arrived at our homes, we told our parents about the nice guys we had just met, how they were polite and not rude.

Both sets of parents decided they too would like to meet up with the guys.

I said to my mum, "Do you want me to bring them over for coffee?"

She replied, "Not yet! We will have coffee in town."

I squealed with delight and was so excited, I couldn't wait for my mum to meet them! I called Eleanor to tell her my news and she also said that her parents wanted to meet the guys as well. The next day, I went to work with a spring in my step with a huge soppy grin on my face and my boss asked me if I was feeling ok. I replied that I was fine and that mum, myself, my friend Eleanor and her parents were going to meet up with a couple of nice guys we had met. He looked serious and said, "You should be very careful. Some guys can play nice but only want one thing in the end and it could turn nasty." I promised that I would be very careful. He was so kind to me and so much like an uncle or even a grandfather.

As it was my half day, I left with my boss's warning ringing in my ears. I headed to meet up with everyone in the coffee shop in town. Everything was going very well. Mum was chatting to Jacques for most of the afternoon asking all sorts of questions. Eleanor's dad was the same, chatting away with Alex. Later in the afternoon, after the guys had left, I sat down with my mum and asked her what she really thought of him?

She said, "He seems like a nice enough young man, Heather Ann. Why do you ask?"

I replied, "In case I fall for him and start to love him."

She frowned and said, "All I can say to you is that you must be very careful. You know what holiday romances are like. They go back home, and they forget all about you. Plus, you also must be careful with your heart too. I mean don't rush into anything with him. You should save yourself, as one day you may meet the man of your dreams! Your heart will be sorted and then you can have a family by all means. Do you understand what I am saying to you, Heather Ann?"

I glumly replied, "Yes, Mum, I do understand every word you are saying to me."

My life was all about my heart. I felt I couldn't do anything apart from keeping my heart safe. It just wasn't fair! I just wanted to be normal like the other girls. We continued to see the guys every day. Jacques, Alex, Eleanor and I were still meeting up at the caravan park. After I had been at work all day my mum said to me, "You know those lads that yourself and Eleanor introduced us to? They seemed like nice lads. You should both bring them over to our house where we could give them a proper Highland welcome and hospitality." They would be offered drinks and dinner. I was thrilled and called Eleanor right away. She was as excited as well.

So, the very next day, we met as usual at the caravan park. I mentioned to them that my mum wants to invite them both to dinner at my house. They were over the moon about it. They said that they would like that very much.

So, I said, "I'll tell my mum and let you know when it's ok for you to come over." We sat on the grassy embankment and chatted excitedly about what it would be like having dinner together.

Alex went and got his football and said, "Would you like to play footy with us?"

We agreed. We were playing a game on the beach where I got very breathless at which I said that I'm not very good at this, but Eleanor was doing brilliantly with the ball and the three of them played on for a while. As the daylight began to fade, we all sat back on the embankment and chatted away for a few hours. We decided that it was time to go home, and the boys decided that they would walk us up the road to the village. We left them at the entrance to the caravan park and walked towards home. Eleanor waved "Cheerio!" As I approached the front gate, my mum was at the front door and said, "You're home then?"

I replied, "Yes, it's good to be on time for once."

She laughed. "Yes, it is!"

We chatted indoors where she asked me whether I had invited the lads over for dinner. I said, "Yes, and they were over the moon."

"Good," she smiled, "then I will be asking them lots of questions and we'll take it from there."

We had a lovely meal and a good old natter and then I got my stuff ready for work and then went to bed.

The next day, I was so excited that I had a man in my life who I could fall in love with if my feelings were strong enough. But I wasn't sure just yet. Before work, I went to put some washing out on the clothesline and as I was doing this mum came out and began chatting about the two young men.

She said, "Are you falling in love with Jacques at all, Heather Ann?"

My face turned bright red, and I said, "No! He's more of a friend than anything else."

She said, "Are you sure? Because if you are, you must be true to him and tell him all about yourself and your medical problems. You can't ever leave anything out."

I said, "I don't know what love is. I have feelings, but I am not sure what they are or what they mean unless they grow into something special."

She said, "Ok." Then we kissed each other goodnight.

The next day, I went to work as usual feeling quite happy and pleased with myself. I worked hard as normal and when we were on our break, I decided to tell my boss about myself and Eleanor meeting these two lovely guys from Glasgow.

He looked worried. "Oh, Heather, please be very careful with them. Glasgow boys are known troublemakers and we don't want you getting hurt, do we?"

I said, "Why is that Mr Fountain?"

He said, "Just call me Charles. I am only trying to look out for you. That's all. Anything could happen to a nice girl like you."

I said, "Thank you, but I'll be ok."

I carried on with my work after the break and made lots of lovely jewellery and packed it into boxes. It was a great job. I had great enjoyment and fun working. There were friendly people to work with in the shop, then came the day that my mum had arranged for the boys to come to our house for dinner. We met them as usual at the caravan park and brought them up to the cottage. The boys waited outside and knocked on the door. Mum came to the door opened it and welcomed them in. Jacques presented my mum with a bunch of flowers and Alex handed her a box of chocolates.

"Oh!" She said surprised. "This is nice of you both, do take a seat and call me Katie."

Mum sat down with the boys and Eleanor, and I made some tea. We shared the tea while mum marvelled over the flowers and chocolates. *What thoughtful gifts they were,* she thought. Mum excused herself and went off to fix the dinner, I also agreed to help. We left Eleanor in the sitting room to entertain the boys for a wee while. While I was helping mum with the dinner, I said, "Well, what do you think of the boys?"

She said, "They're polite and friendly, but that Jacques looks a hard nut and what is that hanging round his neck?"

I said, "I don't know, but its leather whatever it is."

We got on with making the dinner and then set the table ready for our meal. Mum offered Jacques and Alex a drink with their meal. She asked Jacques what is it that he would like to drink.

He replied, "Either beer or whisky, Katie."

She said, "Oooh, a man after my own heart, who loves whisky!"

They both shared a dram together and Alex had a beer. He was a true beer lover. The girls had vodka with coke. Mum began by asking Jacques what is that leather pouch around your neck? He smiled and said, "If I showed you, you would run away from me?"

"Try me," she said. So, Jacques undid the pouch and took it off. He opened it up and showed us all.

"Oh, my Lord! Why are you carrying that around? Especially around your neck, if you got stopped by the police, then what?"

"I use this for shaving! It's my cutthroat blade. It's never used for anything else. Heather and Eleanor, you have nothing to fear. I would never use it to harm anyone especially not you, my darling." He smiled again at my mum.

We believed him as he was so serious when he mentioned it. Mum and the guys got on really well. Laughing and joking all night. It was a brilliant night. It lasted well until the early hours. The boys excused themselves and thanked us all for a wonderful night and headed off down to the caravan park slightly tipsy. We were told to clean up. We cleared up the glasses and plates and did the washing up.

Mum came through and said to us "They're nice lads, you should stick with them." Eleanor wondered whether her parents would be pleased about it too.

Mum said, "Don't you worry, Eleanor, I'll let them know how it went. Don't forget to get their home address before they go back home to Glasgow." So, we took a mental note to ask them the very next time we saw them. We all said goodnight to each other.

Eleanor hugged my mum and said, "Thank you, Katie, for dinner and drinks."

Mum said, "You're very welcome. See you tomorrow."

Chapter 4
First Love?

The next day, Jacques called round and announced that his parents were coming up to Dornoch to stay in a caravan for a wee holiday. They would so much like to meet you. My mum asked him, "How many people are coming to the caravan?"

"There's only the two of them, mum and dad."

"Oh, that will be nice to meet them," Mum said.

Jacques went on, "I was telling them all about you. They're both looking forward to meeting you and your wonderful daughter Heather."

"I must get something nice in to have with a cup of tea and also something special for dinner, that's if they're both up for it?"

He said "Do you mind if I use your telephone? I will give you money for the call. I just want to check what time they're leaving and approximately what time they will arrive here."

"Of course, you can, Jacques, no need for money it's only Glasgow after all." *Such a nice polite young man*, mum thought to herself. He excitedly dialled the number and his mum answered. They were chatting for ages, and he was relaying what his mother was saying. They would arrive in Dornoch the next day at midday, as they must check in to the caravan by 2 p.m. Jacques handed the phone to my mum, and she began exchanging pleasantries over the phone. She said that she was looking forward to meeting them both tomorrow. Jacques, their son, had told me a lot about them, such a lovely polite young man. His mum replied that she hoped it was all good. They both laughed. Mum had a huge beaming smile over her face as she told his mum about the meeting tomorrow.

"So, what do you think?"

"Great that's a definite then. See you both tomorrow." Mum turned to us both as she replaced the receiver and said they were both delighted to be invited over for a cuppa and a meal.

Jacques, Alex, Eleanor, and I excused ourselves and went down to the beach. We went and sat on the sand dunes and began chatting about our lives and what the future could hold for us.

Eleanor decided that she was too afraid to move away from Dornoch, where her family and friends all were, and it would be too scary. She would be very homesick leaving all her friends and she would miss her parents too much.

As for me, I had hard choices to make. I wanted to move away from Dornoch to see if I can find a better life, because to be honest, Dornoch is like a ghost town in winter. There's never anything to do. But a big city could offer so much more. Dornoch is fine in the summer as everywhere is open and there are more visitors. I will miss the beach, of course, and my mum. But I wouldn't be going to the other end of the world. There's so much of this country I haven't seen yet. I would love to be able to come home for weekends too if it's possible.

We sat quietly afterwards, just looking at the calm sea and daydreaming. I said to Jacques "What do you think of the beach and the sea? It's lovely here." he said. "So peaceful. Nothing like where we stay, there's no beach just houses and a few parks."

The sea was so calm. Our minds were as calm as the water. Our eyes shone as blue as the sky on a summer's day. Jacques was getting close to me, but I didn't feel like he was taking advantage of me. He said that he was waiting for the right girl and the right time for both of us. We sat comfortably together for a while until Jacques suggested that we go for a ride on his motorbike.

"Yes please!" I jumped up and hugged him. I just love motorbikes, the hum and roar of the engine and the freedom of the road. I said that one day I am going to get my motorbike licence. He said that we could ride out together and it would be great. I readily agreed. After our ride, Jacques dropped me home and said he would see me later. I went indoors and found mum had left me a note. She had gone to work in the jail craft shop. I decided to go up and see her. She was busy baking scones and cakes. She explained to me that she wouldn't be too much longer and asked if I could do her a huge favour and go back home and put the fire on. I would have to set it and get the coal ready and make dinner for the both of us. Of course, I agreed to do this for my mum, after all, she had been working all day and been on her feet for hours. I thought it would be nice for her to come home and relax, put her feet up and have her dinner sat by the fire listening to the News and Weather and watching her favourite soaps on the TV: Emmerdale, Coronation Street and Murder, she wrote before settling for the night.

So, off I went up the road to do our fire. I got out the kindling and old newspaper to rip up and make into balls. I had to empty the grate of all the old ashes and clean it up then re set the fire. I tried several times to light the fire even using firelighters until at last it took; I used an old newspaper to draw the fire up the chimney until it roared. When the fire was well alight the water in the immersion tank was piping hot. This was the only way to heat our boilers back then.

Mum returned home and was delighted with everything I had done, the roaring fire and a cosy home. I had also made her favourite meal of Mince and tatties, with rice pudding for dessert with jam on top. I offered to wash up and told mum to go through to the sitting room and put her feet up. She looked at me with a huge smile and spoke

"Heather Ann, you are such a loving caring girl, you will go far if you put your mind to it." She gave me one big hug and a kiss on the cheek.

I remember saying, "Thank you, Mum, for your kind words, they mean a lot to me."

Later that evening after the soaps, we sat and had a wee chat. She asked me, "What do you think of Jacques? And be honest."

I said that I liked him and we're both Geminis. We have the same interests, but even though he is so hard on the outside he is as soft as putty on the inside.

She said, "Well, if you like that kind of thing then I will not stand in your way. But Heather Ann, the only thing I am worried about is your heart. Your heart problems take over most of your life, which you know and should understand that this is serious because if anything happens to you it could be

62

to do with your heart. I love you so very much and don't want anything bad to happen to you, this would destroy me."

I paused then said, "Mum! I'm not a soft touch, Jacques knows about my heart problems and he's ok with that."

"I sure hope he does!" she said.

While getting ready for bed I said to mum, "Are you looking forward to tomorrow? Meeting the parents and everything?"

She replied, "It's very quick wanting to meet the parents, you've only known him for a wee while? But I suppose it's ok as they're already coming here for a wee holiday anyway, why not?"

We hugged and said goodnight. No sooner had I put my head on the pillow, I drifted off into a deep sleep dreaming about the next day.

I awoke early to the sound of the hoover going. I jumped out of bed with a startle and went downstairs, where mum was busy doing housework.

I said, "Mum, what are you doing? It's far too early to be hoovering!" I offered to help, but mum was having none of it. She said that I had to go back upstairs and make myself look presentable for our visitors, then come back down and prepare breakfast for the both of us. So excitedly I ran back upstairs, doing what I was told, had a wash, and put a summer dress on and made myself look pretty. I then went back downstairs and prepared a lovely breakfast for us. I told my mum to take off her housework clothes for the wash and put something lovely on and make yourself look nice. I liked when she put her blonde hair up in a bun.

She muttered something about me being cheeky and went and did as she was told. When she returned, looking as lovely as ever, we shared breakfast together. Mum had her blue eyeliner on, which brought out her blue eyes bigger, with her blonde hair all tidy and very nice. I said that I was so very proud of her and how lovely she looked in her pretty dress.

Alex and Jacques were walking up the path towards the cottage and rapped on the door. I answered and invited them both inside. Jacques smiled and spoke

"Wow! You both look very nice. Are you going out somewhere nice and posh?"

I smiled and said, "No. We're just dressed up for your mum and dad coming over to visit. When will they be arriving to come and see us?"

Jacques said that they had already arrived and were both over at the caravan site resting after the drive up. They were both looking forward to meeting us.

Mum said, "We're looking forward to meeting them very much too, Jacques."

Mum asked the boys to take a seat and offered them a cup of tea and some cake which she had baked specially for the occasion. They readily agreed and we sat and had a blether. Conversation was around how long they were staying on the caravan site? They said that they were going back soon, before Jacques' mum and dad as they had to get back to work. Jacques asked mum if I could go back with them too. Just to see life from a different place and see if I liked it. I might like to do my nursing training down in Glasgow?

Mum looked stern and just said, "I haven't met your mum and dad yet, but I can discuss that with them if that's what you would like to do Heather as it's not your place, it's theirs."

Jacques smiled a weak smile and said, "Of course, I understand that. Yes, that's fine. They will be up this evening Katie, to see you and of course, the lovely Heather too."

I blushed and went all coy.

Mum asked Jacques how long they were up for. He replied that they were just here for a week, a break from home and work. The boys excused themselves and went off out to do their own thing as they had a few things to do before the meeting with his parents. Eleanor knocked at the door just as they were leaving, and the three of us sat down with a fresh cuppa and had a blether.

Mum told Eleanor what Jacques had said. Eleanor was a wee bit shocked but said that he didn't seem the sort of lad who would take advantage of me, especially because of my heart problems.

Mum said, "He had better not take advantage of my girl or I will rip his balls off and feed them to him! I will shred him to bits and do time for it! No one takes advantage of my daughter the way she is!"

Eleanor looked shocked and stifled a giggle. She had never heard my mum ever talk like that before.

I was very quiet, thinking to myself. *Why is it always my heart problems taking over my life like that? Is there no way in this world to get a better life than always watching my heart?*

Mum looked at me all worried and said, "You're very quiet, my girl. What's wrong with you?"

I said, "I'm fine, don't be worrying about me all the time. Mum, you have looked after me all these years. Please let me have some space now to look after myself, without you worrying all the time. I am a grown woman now; I should know the difference between what is right or wrong."

Mum just looked hurt but said nothing just began humming to herself with songs.

I said to Eleanor as I took her aside, "I wish she would just drop it about my heart all the time."

Eleanor said, "It's just because she cares about you. If she didn't care, she would just let you go off and do whatever you want to do."

I took Eleanor over to the door and said that I would see her tomorrow and we hugged, and she went off down the path. As I was closing the door, mum said it won't be long before Jacques' mum and dad Isa and Robert will be coming over to see us.

"Is he coming with them?"

I said, "No, it's your time to meet up and get to know each other and mine too."

I went up to my room to tidy it up. I just sat on the bed with tears in my eyes and said to myself, "Why do I have that stupid heart problem, why can't it just go away so I can get better and get on with my life? Every time there is an opening in my life the heart situation seems to stop it!"

At that moment, I felt a breeze from the window and yet there was no wind outside all was calm and still. I looked up puzzled as to how that happened. Was there someone else there listening to what I had to say? For that moment, it was intense, peaceful, and yet calming. But I was alone in my room…

So, I pulled myself together and got on with my tidying, going through my old stuff, until I heard both a knock at the door and the doorbell ringing.

I looked out of the window and there was a posh car on the street outside. Mum answered the door and put on a posh voice to match. It was Jacques' parents Isa and Robert each introducing the other. I could hear mum talking out loud saying that she had heard a lot about them both from their delightful polite son Jacques. I heard Isa say that she hoped it was all good and they all laughed. "I've heard a lot about you and your lovely daughter Heather." Mum invited them into the sitting room, and they all began chatting loudly. "So, tell me, Katie, where is Heather? I would love to meet her. Jacques was talking about her so much and he's very much taken with her."

"Yes?" Mum said, "Heather too, I'm afraid. She is upstairs tidying up her room, but she will be down soon."

So, Isa and Robert were chatting away in good style, and they were getting along well. Finally, I had finished what I was doing in my room, and I calmly walked down the stairs wondering what to expect. There they all were sat in the sitting room, like long lost friends all chatting together.

A lovely couple they were. Isa and Robert looked up and smiled. Mum introduced me as Heather Ann, a bone of contention of mine but that's my name! Isa and Robert introduced themselves too and we all sat down together. Isa began by saying how bonny I looked and then asked how did I meet her son? I said that we were down at the caravan park, and they just came over for a chat.

Isa said, "Oh! He's told me a lot about you. He never shuts up about you!"

"I hope it's all good?" I asked.

Laughing, she said, "Yes, of course!"

Isa continued, "I'm happy, in fact we're so happy to meet you and your mum. It's nice to put faces to names."

We had a lovely meal together and the couple congratulated Mum on her cooking skills. They offered to do the dishes, but Mum refused saying that they were guests. We had a brilliant evening and unfortunately soon it was over.

We all said our goodbyes with hugs and handshakes, and they were off into the night, to return to their caravan.

The next day, as mum was getting ready for work, I asked if there was anything she needed me to do in the house before I went out? She gave me a long list of things to do. I felt like I was Cinderella working in the house! I was washing dishes, setting the fire, polishing, and hoovering before I could go to the ball, or rather go out!

After I had done all the housework, I went up to see Eleanor. She was inside with her mum and dad. They asked me how I was, and I just said, "I'm fine, how are you?" They said that they had heard that we had met some fine young men at the caravan park.

I said, "Yes, we have. They're both from Glasgow." Eleanor's parents said that we need to be very careful as some of the Glasgow ones who come up here on holidays just use the local lassies and then just leave them for dead with no further contact.

I said, "We are very careful!"

We excused ourselves and headed off for the caravan park.

As we approached the caravan park, we saw Jacques standing outside his mum and dad's caravan. He looked up and noticed us and called us over. His mum and dad were sitting outside on their chairs. They got up and gave us both a big hug. "You must be Eleanor!" Isa beamed. "I'm Jacques's mum Isa and this is Robert his dad." I was puzzled as to why the big hug. But Isa said, "This is to welcome you into the family, Heather." We all sat down around the table and had a proper blether, and we had a nice time.

"My son tells me that he has been asking you to come down to Glasgow for a month or two to see if you like it," Isa enquired.

I replied, "Yes, just to see if I like it and to have a job down there too for a different kind of life."

"Why?" She asked, "Aren't you happy where you are?"

I told her that I needed to see other parts of Scotland.

She agreed that it would be nice, but it was up to my mum as well as me. I nodded in agreement. Robert and Isa were on board with the idea.

Mum said to me. "Now, Heather Ann, you are to go down the road to Glasgow where Jacques will meet you and take you back to his parents' house."

So, I packed a few things into a holdall bag. I chose a big bag, so that if I bought clothes down in Glasgow, I could bring them back with me. I was so excited that night I couldn't sleep. Mum was still up having a hot drink. So, I asked if I could join her, and we sat and had a wee chat over a hot drink of cocoa.

She was surprised to see me and asked what the matter was. I said, "I'm excited to go, but I'm also rather nervous. What if something bad happens?"

She smiled and said, "My dear daughter, I'm sure that you will be fine, but as always, my door will always be open for you, and you will always have a room here."

We hugged and shed a few tears. Mum also said that she had already given my savings book to Isa to hold onto for me so as if I needed something it's there for me to fall back on. I thanked my mum and said it meant a lot for her to think of me. She ushered me up to bed saying I needed to get plenty of sleep as I had a long journey to go on in the morning. I lay on my bed wondering what it would be like and how scary it was leaving home for the first time ever. Pretty soon I fell into a deep sleep.

I woke to the sound of the droning alarm at 6.30 a.m. Bleary eyed, I went to the bathroom got washed and dressed and headed downstairs. The smell was amazing, mum was in the kitchen making me a cooked breakfast of Bacon, Lorne sausage, tattie scone, black pudding, egg, mushrooms, and fried bread. I was surprised in a nice way and said,

"Oh, my goodness, Mum! Why have you done all of this for me?"

She replied, "You are my only daughter and I need to feed you up before you go. I don't want you to be hungry on the journey and spending your money on things you don't need to."

After I had eaten my delicious breakfast and drank my cup of tea, I got up from the table and was ready to go. Mum said that she would walk with me to the bus stop and see me off. There was an unspoken bond between us as we walked down the road. We were both quite teary eyed and neither of us wanted to say how we felt.

As we walked down the road, we met mum's friend Joan, who was a cleaner at the local academy. She looked surprised to see us walking at that time in the morning. She asked me where I was off to. I explained that I was off down the road to Glasgow to stay with my friend and hopefully find a job down there to move on with my life. She wished me all the luck in the world, going down there at such a young age.

I gave my mum a big hug. "I love you, Mum, please look after yourself while I'm away. I'll make sure to keep in touch!"

So, the bus was getting ready to go. I had tears welling up in my eyes, but I tried to be brave, as mum said we were only saying Au Revoir and not goodbye. When I got to my seat, I was shaking with excitement but also very scared at the thought of leaving home. Mum was waving, wiping tears from her eyes, and she looked a lonely, old lady, who kept her eyes on the bus until it left her sight, and headed towards Inverness.

The journey seemed to last an age but soon we arrived in Inverness, and I got off the bus and trudged into the train station to board the train heading for Glasgow where Jacques would be meeting me. As the train jolted and began to move off for the long journey to my new home, I picked up a book I had brought from home, when a fine young man sat down opposite me. He smiled as I looked up from my book and enquired as to where I was going.

I told him that I was heading for Glasgow. He looked at me with a stern face and said, "You should be very careful, it isn't a safe place for such a young girl!" I told him that I was meeting a friend down there and staying with him and his parents for a while. He just smiled and mumbled something under his breath. He was nice and polite, and we chatted about how nice the weather had been and where we both came from.

It wasn't long before he said that it was his stop next. He was heading for Stirling for work, and he arose from his seat with his briefcase. He wished me luck and said, "Stay safe, there are plenty of bad men out there just looking for young ones." After he had walked to the door and got off the train. I felt a shiver down my spine and his words gave me the creeps.

The rest of the journey wasn't very long but it felt so very lonely on my own in the carriage. The train arrived in Glasgow in the late afternoon and as we pulled in my frown turned to a nervous smile as I saw a friendly face standing on the platform waiting for me. It was Jacques and I was so happy to see him. He took my bag, and we chatted as we left the station.

It was so nice to be with someone I knew, and he was asking how the journey was, I said that it was fine but very long and lonely. As we walked across the car park, I saw his motorbike and asked excitedly if we were going to his house on the bike? He nodded smiling. I took my bag and strapped it to my back, and he gave me a full-face helmet and he sat on the bike, helping me get my leg over the seat and he said, "Hold on tight!" and away we went. It was some ride. I gripped him tightly all the way.

We soon arrived at his parents' house and what a lovely house it was, or so I thought. It wasn't a house at all, but a two-bedroomed flat. The rooms were very spacious, and he took me to his room. I asked him, "Where would I be sleeping?"

He said that I was to have his room and he would be on the couch as he wasn't one to take advantage of a young woman. He wasn't like that. I smiled and thanked him. "You're so kind." His parents were not in when we arrived, and I asked when they would be back? He told me that they would be away for a few days. So, we had the flat to ourselves. In his room he had a skull and a mixture of sprays and gels.

He asked me if I wanted to meet his mates. So, I agreed and off we went on his bike. Oh Lord! When we arrived, they looked tough with leather jackets, leather trousers and tattoos. They looked like real hard nuts. Jacques could see I was scared but he reassured me that they wouldn't hurt me, or he would have something to say. So, I felt much calmer with them, and they were all so nice to me. We all went on the bikes around the streets of Glasgow for a ride and it was great fun. When we arrived back at the flat, he made me some food, which was really tasty. After the meal I was very tired. So, I wished him goodnight and went to my room. As I looked around the room, I saw a few pictures on the table of Eleanor and myself. I smiled and thought that was nice that he thought of us.

The next morning, I awoke to the sound of a telephone ringing in the sitting room. I came out and asked Jacques who it was, and he just said that was my ma and da, they're cutting short their holiday and coming back home. He laughed and said I don't think they trust us alone together. His sister came over and spent some time with us. Her name was Paige, and she was lovely and bubbly. We chatted for a while. She asked me, "Why down here of all places?" I simply said to see if Jacques and I can make a go of it with a relationship, as we are such close friends. Also, I wanted to try and see if I can find work in nursing or anything to earn money and make a career.

She told me there were no nursing jobs there in Larkhall only in Glasgow Royal Infirmary. That's quite a way from here and I would have to pay for my digs, which wouldn't leave me with much money. I was downhearted but decided to stay for a few weeks anyway to see if anything was available to suit me, if not, I would return home to Dornoch.

Almost a month had passed, and I still hadn't found a suitable job. I decided to have a wee chat with Isa and Robert, saying that I didn't think it's working out for me in Glasgow or a relationship with him, as I had hoped, but we'll still stay good friends. I want to return home to Dornoch. As I went to get my train ticket, I still had bad chest pains, but was still taking the medication prescribed by the doctors in the highlands. Jacques and I grabbed some time alone to have a wee chat. I explained to him "There will be no future for us when we are separated, and you won't leave Glasgow for the highlands." So, we decided to part as good friends, which was the best option. He wasn't very happy and offered to do more, but we finally admitted that it wouldn't work.

We walked back to the flat arm in arm, still struggling to cope with the situation, but we had agreed and there was no more to be said. We were both puffy eyed but still happy to be friends.

That night, Isa had made us a very nice meal with a few drinks. We had a lovely final evening together all talking about how lovely the last few weeks had been and what a shame it was that I thought it best to go back to Dornoch.

The next morning, I woke early and headed into the lounge. Isa was in the kitchen, cooking breakfast for us all. As we ate breakfast, Isa and Robert said they would take me to the train station and Jacques would meet us there. Isa gave me the bank book my mum had secretly given her. I was shocked.

"Gosh. If I knew that you had this, I would have asked for it."

Isa smiled and said that she had made a promise to my mum to keep it safe for me until I really needed it.

"We have all enjoyed having you staying with us, and I wish you all the happiness in the world. May God Bless you wherever you go. Please keep in touch with us. It would be lovely to hear from you."

Jacques hugged me with teary eyes and Robert gave me a fatherly hug and a wee handshake. We all had said our goodbyes and they waved until I went onto the platform and onto the train. I pulled up the window of the door on the train and waved goodbye, as tears filled my eyes.

Sadly, I walked to one of the carriage rooms and sat down staring out of the window with tears of sadness and tears of joy stinging my eyes. My heart was cut in two. I didn't want to leave but knew I must. I missed my mum too and I looked forward to seeing her. Robert, Isa and Jacques were like family to me, but I needed to go further. It was like someone was saying this is not for you. The journey to Inverness was an uneventful one; with tear-soaked cheeks, I got on the bus back to Dornoch with a heavy heart, but also with joy, as I was going home to see my mum. I arrived in Dornoch in darkness and ran into my mum's arms. Mum held me tightly and dried my tears, then took me home and made me supper. We hugged and cried together.

After supper, we sat down and had a wee chat over a cocoa, just like the night I left. "What happened, Heather Ann?"

"There are no jobs down there suitable for me. I didn't feel comfortable living there. I really needed my own space. Isa and Robert were very good to me, but it was not the same.

As for Jacques, he was too full of himself, and I didn't think that it would work out. So, we parted as good friends."

Mum just smiled and said, "Well, at least you're home now, until you make another decision on what you want to do with your life."

Chapter 5
England Revisited

At some point later, mum had two weeks holidays to take from work. She suggested that we have a wee break away from home in Embo. She asked me whether I would like to go to England for a holiday, to see the place where I was born and where my Aunt Janet was looking after me when I was a wee baby? "What do you say to that, my girl?" I told mum that I would love that very much as I hadn't been to Ipswich since my early years. We were both looking forward to leaving home and going on a big adventure together.

I went off on a tangent, talking about if I liked it then maybe I may stay down there and who knows, get a part-time job, and save money to do a course in nursing to follow in my mum's footsteps.

I really must have been intolerable, as I kept asking Mum loads of questions about England.

Mum said that we would be getting a train from Inverness and the ticket man is lovely and friendly enough to chat with. "Also, Heather Ann, when you arrive at the border of Scotland, the train slows down and stops at Carlisle, where they switch drivers."

"Oh my Lord! Wow! Mum, what happens then?"

Mum said, "You must stay in your seat, as you get jostled about. The train, instead of rocking gently feels like it's going like the clappers, a bat out of hell, if you wish. It goes so fast that you wonder whether the train will stay on the track or not. It's like the driver is rushing home to his wife, as she is warming the bed for him!"

I just sat and stared. "You have got to be kidding? Really?"

She started to shake and then she just laughed aloud.

"Yes, mum, I understand, but I don't believe you."

She just continued laughing.

"Oh, and plus, when you arrive in London at Euston Station, everyone is always in a rush and so busy. But if they find out you're a stranger there are some people who would take advantage of you. So, be careful who you chat to and always keep an eye on your handbag."

After hearing this, I was still quite excited, and nothing would put me off. I was looking forward so much to going away.

While my mum was working very hard, and as her boss was away on holiday, I decided that I would get over to the shop where she was working to volunteer to help.

Mum was delighted with my help.

Mum loved her job at the Co-Op. There was a new manager in charge there, Noel and his wife was called Vera. They were very friendly and came from Leicester. Just now, they were on holiday, and we were allowed to use their house rather than travel to and from Embo all the time. This was fantastic as the house was attached to the shop. Mum also had a few other jobs to do as well as the Co-Op. She was a caretaker for a local social club, where the people enjoyed playing Whist drives and other community activities. She was also still helping dressing the dead through the night. On her days off, she worked for Grannies Heilan Hame in Embo, which is a caravan and holiday park owned by her friend and employer John Mackintosh. They got on well and he was always kind to me. She was always busy earning money to pay the bills.

I tried to help with the different jobs mum had but didn't want to get pay for it as it was better for my mum to get the full wage.

At some point, it was time to get ready and start packing as it won't be too long until we're going on holiday.

We were so excited and couldn't wait to go. Eleanor came over to see me and was asking me how it went when I was down the road in Glasgow with Jacques and his parents. I told her that he was always acting the hard man and I would not be going with him, as that's not my sort of guy. I was not in love with him like that; we were just friends. He was like a brother to me. His mum and dad were darlings and had said that any time I wanted to go down to see them, their door was always open. Eleanor agreed that she thought he was too full of himself and his own self-importance. But he was such a nice guy. His mum and dad seemed very nice and friendly. She asked, "What are your plans now that it's not going to be Glasgow?"

I told her that mum and I were going away for two weeks for a holiday. If I liked it, I might be able to stay and find a career down there. Eleanor smiled and looked surprised. She said, "Wow! Anywhere nice?" I replied saying that it was where I was born in England. A place called Ipswich. Also, to the seaside resort called Felixstowe where my Aunt Janet used to look after me. She smiled and told me that sounded lovely.

"It would be nice to get away and spread your wings. I wish I was like you, but I'm a home bird and couldn't bear to be away from my friends and family for too long."

As for me, I could never be like that stuck at home with adventure.

As our holiday approached, mum had to let the people who were renting our home in Embo know the contact details for the place we would be staying in England if there were any problems. As it was packing day, we were busy sorting clothing for the large case. We checked we had our tickets and money sorted; as the English were funny about Scottish banknotes, we had to get English notes instead. I was so excited and couldn't really settle. My brother Jonas had come to the house while he was on leave from his new job on the oil rigs out in the North Sea near Norway. He said that he thought we were 'both mad and needed our bumps felt going down there.'

Mum argued back, "We are nothing of the sort! Heather wanted to see where she was born and to visit Felixstowe where your Aunt Janet used to look after her and take her out as a baby before I returned back home to Scotland. What's wrong with that? You were only a young boy at the time."

He must have thought better of replying that and wished us both a safe journey and stay safe. He used our bath and took a meal from mum and then went back to his wife.

Cheek of him!

We went to bed all excited, but sleep fled far from us.

The next morning, we were up very early as we had to catch the 8.30 a.m. bus from the Dornoch main bus stop. The train was due to leave Inverness at 10 a.m. No sooner had the bus pulled into the bus station, we were off walking quickly towards the train station. We were in luck, the train was already in. However, the station was very busy and amidst all the jostling and many people vying for a good seat, we managed to get on the train and into our seats. After we had put our suitcase away and began to relax, the ticket collector appeared with a cheery smile and a deep, "Hello, tickets please."

He checked our tickets and asked us where we were going? We told him our destination was Ipswich and Felixstowe. He pursed his lips and said, "Phew! That's a long way. Have a lovely and safe journey."

We relaxed and sank back into the plush British Rail seats and looked out of the window as the train pulled out of the station. The scenery was spectacular.

The journey was easy, and the train quietly sped along the track and mum suddenly said that I should go with her as we were approaching Edinburgh. I wondered where she was taking me. The train was nearing the Forth Bridge and mum gave me some coins and as the train stopped to wait for the lights to change. She said to throw the coins from the window into the Firth. "But before you do, make a wish and it will come true." So, I did as I was told, and I noticed a few other people were doing the same. I was pleased with myself and returned to our seats and started to read my book and eventually, went to sleep, dreaming about my wish to see if it would come true.

The journey was very long and as we approached the border with England, the ticket man came and said Carlisle next stop.

I turned to mum and said, "Carlisle, isn't that England?"

"Yes, Heather Ann, and here's where they change drivers and take the bags of letters from the train."

I asked, "Why do they have to change drivers?"

Mum said that the Scottish driver had done his bit and he needed a break to unwind.

As the new driver entered his cab, the guard blew his whistle, and we slowly left the station. The train started to pick up speed even my bag started to slide in front of me. I asked mum, "Why is he driving so fast?" She laughed until her whole body trembled into a fit of giggles as she laughingly said, "Maybe to get home to his wife, as she will be keeping the bed warm for him!"

The new ticket inspector came to ask to inspect our tickets and he said,

"Oh! From Scotland? You have both had a long journey?"

I looked at him and sulked, "It was not as fast as this driver."

He grinned and clipped our tickets and moved on through the train. The journey continued apace, and it wasn't too long until we arrived at Euston Station in London. Mum said we had to get a move on as we had to get off this train to catch the connecting one across a few platforms for Ipswich.

We dashed through the station and just made it onto the train when the guard's whistle signalled the train's departure. "Phew!" The journey from London to Ipswich wasn't long at all. No sooner had we got our breath back after the run for the train in Euston Station, the ticket inspector shouted, "Ipswich, next stop. End of the line. All change."

We had just left the train and were standing at the taxi rank just outside. When a taxi finally arrived, we got in with our luggage and mum told the driver an address and off we went. Before long, we arrived at a house with a lovely garden and a well-kept porchway. Mum said I was to behave myself as this was an old friend of hers from her nursing days. The lady was lovely, she made us very welcome indeed. She asked us to sit, and she brought us a tray with tea and some sandwiches and a wee cake each. Mum and the lady were chatting about the good old days. As the night was getting on, we finished our tea and food and excused ourselves. We were led to a twin room with two single beds, and we got ready for bed. Mum said if I liked it here, I could come home for the rest of my stuff and then move down and stay here with this lady until I could find some new digs. I said that we should wait and see what happens. So, with that, we bid each other goodnight and drifted off into a long-awaited deep slumber. Filled with memories of the train journey and dreams of what Felixstowe would bring tomorrow.

The next day, we were feeling well-rested and were presented with a lovely breakfast. Mum spoke to the lady and said that we would return later. So, off we went on the bus to Felixstowe, a seaside town on the East Coast about 12 miles from Ipswich.

It was a lovely day, and we were walking along the promenade, when mum spotted yet another old friend from her nursing days. They both hugged and kissed each other's cheek, both wiped away tears from their faces. The lady called my mum Cathy, saying how lovely it was to be seeing each other again and how delighted she was to meet me. We decided to walk along with the lady, and she gave us a grand tour of Felixstowe. As we neared the port, the lady said there were the ferries which travelled to Holland and Zeebrugge,

Belgium. They were always on the go and always busy with passengers. I noticed both ships names. One was called the Viking Voyager and the sister ship was the Herald of Free Enterprise. *Such a mouthful*, I thought. They were both marked as Townsend Thoresen. They looked enormous and standing proud on the dockside. I said to mum, "I would love to go on one of them for a wee trip and get duty-free ciggys and stuff to take home." She nodded and decided to get tickets for it. I was very excited as mum went to buy the tickets for the trip the next day. My mum's friend told us both to make ourselves at home and then go on the Townsend Thoresen and come back and tell her all about it. She was working on the prom in an amusement arcade. It was her business, and she had a large family. Her boys were regularly put in charge, and they were run off their feet as it was a busy season.

Later that evening, mum and I were walking along the beach chatting together and saying how lovely it was. We walked over to look at the shops and decided to have a fish supper, before trudging back onto the beach to eat it. It was a lovely warm night. As we sat there eating, we were watching the Townsend Thoresen ship coming into the port. Mum said, "If you're planning to move down here, I would be sorry to see you go, and I'd miss you very much, you're my only girl." I took her arm and told her not to say anymore as she would make me cry. She asked me "Why would you cry? I'm just being honest."

I told her, "I thought that you loved my brother Jonas more than me, since he's your first born and doesn't cause any problems. As for me, since I have come into this world, I have caused you so much worry with my heart and all. Not being

84

able to do much schooling and causing you so much grief with the way I have been with boys."

She turned to me with a tearful gaze and shook her head with a smile. "Heather Ann, you have never caused me grief and you have done more than your brother Jonas has done. You have helped me out with the shop and helped me make the meals, you help around the house and have done more than he ever did. You didn't help me with dressing the dead as that wasn't for you. So, please don't say you have caused me grief because you haven't. Jonas did certain things for me, but you have done so much more. Now, he is with that woman, and she has taken my son away from me."

She continued, "So, my darling Heather Ann, I am so grateful for what you have done and are doing for me. If you did decide to live here, then you will have my blessing."

We hugged and walked back to mum's friend's house. We sat up for a while and had a few drinks, then went to bed happy. The morning soon came and after breakfast, we packed a wee bag, checked our tickets and our passports. Mum said Cheerio to her friend and as we waved goodbye, she wished us Bon Voyage. We were both so excited, like wee children off on an adventure. As we approached the gang plank, the ship looked so huge, and we shakily walked on board. What a lovely ship it was! The name Viking Voyager was written on all the life buoys and life rafts. We were having a lovely time. The ship was full of Scottish football players. We ran up to the top deck and leaned on the rails, watching the ship pull out of Felixstowe dock into the North Sea. The crew worked hard for us all, making sure everyone was happy. I asked mum, "Would you like a drink?"

"Ooh yes, I would love a whisky to reach my heart." The water was getting rough and choppy, and the boat was rocking.

We sat in the bar and noticed flashing lights and music in the next room—it looked like a disco. We ordered our drinks and mum was watching people staggering around the room as the boat was rocking more wildly than before. Mum downed her whisky and said, "I think I'll get another one."

So, off she went to the bar, I thought she was never coming back. I looked over to the bar and saw her chatting away merrily with the crew. When she came back, the boat was really rocking and she said, "Hell, you would think I was pissed," as she nearly fell over a few times.

I laughed. "You took your time!" What was she doing all that time?

"What on earth were you doing?" I asked inquisitively.

"I was asking whether there were any jobs going for you, since you love Felixstowe, and you are from Scotland. The barman said there are lots of jobs going. Just pick up an application form from the steward and fill it in and we'll take it from there," Mum replied kindly.

A young man came over and asked me if I would like to dance. I was shocked and looked at my mum in fright, as I was very shy. She smiled back at me and said, "What are you waiting for? Go on, he's a crew member."

So, off I went, still embarrassed that he had asked me. As we were dancing, he was asking me lots of questions.

"Your mum says that you would love a job on here, meeting people and welcoming them on-board."

I nodded and shyly said, "I will have to think about it."

He smiled and said, "Here's my address, we can keep in touch with each other, see how you're getting on."

I wrote my address on a piece of paper and gave him it after he gave me his own. I said, "Thank you," and scurried back to mum's table. She had a great big grin on her face.

I said, "What's up with you?"

She smiled and said, "That the guy fancied you!"

"Don't be daft! We're just friends and we've only just met."

She smiled wider and said, "Mmm. Friends can turn into lovers," and I blushed brightly. We relaxed and watched everyone else trying to stand upright and making fools of themselves. We ordered food and had a lovely meal. Mum indicated we should go up on deck as we were going to be in Zeebrugge soon. So, we went on deck and the wind was dying down. This majestic ship pulled into the dock, and we watched as people were disembarking and re-boarding the ship. We saw quite a few women standing on the dockside and I asked one of the crew who were they and what were they waiting for?

He said, "They are ladies of the night. They come down to see if they can earn money from unsuspecting crew and passengers."

I said, "What for?" Mum told me to hush.

He said, "They're not good women—wanting sex like that."

"Oh," I said blushing.

"Would you like to have a look around the ship, as it's your first time aboard?" I looked at Mum and she smiled saying, "Thank you," and we both excitedly followed him. We were taken to the bridge and introduced to the captain who was very polite and was telling us all about his ship and how many passengers they can carry. He also said that there are several crew members down in the boiler room of mixed nationalities. He made us feel very special and very welcome on-board. He allowed us to take photos with him to take back to Scotland and show them all what it was like. We went to the shop on-board and bought some duty-free cigarettes as Jonas and his wife Leslie were smokers. Mum bought me a bottle with a ship inside it as a keepsake. We walked back to our same seats. The crew gave us blankets to keep warm and sleep with. Mum saw a sign that read 'Station.'

She asked a passing crewman, "What is this station?"

"It's the boiler room, madam," he said. "That's where all the lads work to keep the ship going."

She wanted to see what it was like, so the man opened the door, and all the guys were adjusting dials and knobs and working up a sweat in the steam. They spotted us and all smiled. "This is the heart of the ship, and this is our job," the nearest lad said to us. Mum began chatting away with them about her Navy days. They were very friendly, and mum said they would all be getting a drink from us as a thank you for all their hard work on the ship. They all looked stunned as nobody had offered that before. She noted it all down and said if she saw the captain, she would ask him about why these fine fellows were not being appreciated.

As she was heading for the bar, the captain was already there and asked mum, "Who are all these drinks for?"

She smiled and said, "They're all for me."

He laughed and said, "You're not surely going to be drinking all of that?"

Mum smiled sweetly at him and said, "No, these are for your crew in the boiler room, they deserve a wee drink for all their hard work, and we are not at sea yet."

He smiled back and said, "That's so very kind of you and your daughter."

After speaking with the captain, a crew member was told to help mum down to the boiler room with the drinks for the crew. As she arrived with the drinks, you would have thought that they had won the pools or the lottery as they had never been treated like this before. They were so delighted that the captain had agreed they could have a drink from us.

When we had been talking with the crew for a while, we said our farewells, leaving a happy crew back to work as usual. We decided to visit the duty-free shop on-board once more. I got my duty-free cigarettes and mum went for some whisky. After our shopping, we went up on deck to relax while the new passengers came aboard for the return voyage. I was thinking to myself that it was a busy ship, and I would like to work on it especially as the barman had said they were short staffed. The captain asked me if I would ever consider working on here. I had said that I wouldn't mind as it's only sailing back and forth from Felixstowe to Zeebrugge. So, I turned to mum and asked her what she thought, as I was seriously considering asking for a job.

Mum smiled and said, "If you think you'll like that sort of thing. You will get to meet and greet all sorts of people from all over." I decided not to hang around, so I went straight to the captain and asked him how I go about applying for a job on-board. He had me fill in an application form there and then. He was very pleased and said that he would send for me when he had passed my details on. I was very excited at the prospect of working aboard such a lovely ship with such a lovely friendly crew. My mind was wandering as I was daydreaming about working here. The only other thing I would need to sort out would be board and lodgings in Felixstowe. I was hoping Mum's friend would be able to help me out there.

As the ship slipped slowly away from the dock, the sea was very calm, and mum and I drifted off into a deep sleep on our chairs. I had a lovely dream of my future working on this ship. The return crossing seemed shorter than the original journey and no sooner had I closed my eyes, it was time to disembark. As we had got our belongings together, we decided to go through the green channel, nothing to declare. But mum was stopped and asked to empty her bags. They found the ship in the bottle, and they were both having a laugh about whether she had drunk it all before finding the ship. The sailor was Scottish too. Everything was fine and we were cleared to continue.

As we arrived back at my mum's friend's house, mum excitedly told her that I had applied for a job on the ship! She also suggested that there was a hospital in Felixstowe where I could also get work, as well as St Helen's Hospital in Ipswich. She thought that I could do all my training for the nursing there when I wasn't working on board the ship. I was overjoyed and couldn't wait to come back down to start my new life and career. Mum's friend told her that she had received a phone call while she had been away. Mum returned the call to her friend in Embo, who told her that the tenants of mum's house had trashed it. We sadly told our host that we couldn't stay longer and that we would have to return home as soon as possible.

We thanked her for her hospitality and kindness in putting us up and we hoped to return soon. I hoped that I would be down much sooner. We packed quickly and quietly; I was very solemn as I didn't want to return home. But I had no choice as I was with my mum. We had a nice meal and then went to bed.

The next day, we were up early and had a lovely breakfast, said our farewells, and prepared to catch the bus for Ipswich, followed by the train bound for Euston Station, then Inverness. It was going to be some journey! We hugged mum's friend and she said, "Don't leave it too long next time, Cathy." I was sad on leaving as we had enjoyed our stay even although it had been cut short. We boarded the bus bound for Ipswich and we waved goodbye with tears flowing freely down our faces. It wasn't long on the bus, then we boarded the train, which was very busy bound for London to change again at Euston Station. This proved to be a nightmare as we had to get across a bridge to board the train for Inverness. "Phew! We made it with minutes to spare." We sat down all puffed out and when we were relaxing, Mum said to me that she couldn't do this all the time as it would drive her insane.

As the train increased speed after leaving Euston Station, we were moving at a faster pace and several stations we whipped through, leaving the people on the platforms windswept. We only stopped at a few stations until we arrived at Carlisle. There the driver changed over, and the Scottish driver took over and the train's pace slowed down a wee bit. The train moved slowly through the Scottish countryside, a light pushing on through the darkness until we arrived at Inverness Station in the early hours of the next day. We disembarked and walked through to the bus station to catch a bus for Dornoch and Embo.

As we arrived in Embo, mum said, "Let's go up to the house and see what's happened."

Mum opened the door to the lovely cottage which her father had built with his own hands, and she stood there aghast and burst out in tears. The people who had rented the house had wrecked everything and she didn't know where to start. Everything was ruined. Upstairs and downstairs, the whole cottage was a hell of a mess! I held her hand and stayed with her to help as much as I could. We managed to tidy quite a bit and with the help of some of our friendly neighbours we got it almost back to normal. But then the tiredness began to take its toll and we decided to go to our beds as the day had been a very long and a stressful one.

The next day, we decided to get everything back to normal and I would stay here with her until then. Mum had to return to work the next week and she was glad that I was there to look after the house while she was away. We both knew that it wouldn't be long until I went away and a few weeks later, I decided it was time to leave to go back to Felixstowe. As I was packing my bags to prepare for this big move in my life, mum sat me down and said to me, "Are you sure you want this?"

I said with a determined face, "Yes, more than ever."

Chapter 6
South for the Winter

I got ready to go away to Felixstowe. That morning, we both cried on each other's shoulders. Mum said to me that she would see me off at the bus station.

I cried. "I don't like saying goodbye!"

Mum said, "It's not goodbye, it's until we meet again, but take extra care."

Once more, we hugged and kissed and cried and I got onto the bus for Inverness. Tearfully, I watched mum's sad face with tears streaming down her face trying to force a smile. At Inverness, I got the train to Euston and then to Ipswich. The journeys were all uneventful, plenty of time to think of what lay in my future.

I was due to start as a nursing trainee at St Helen's Hospital. I was excited and everything was going well, and I was making many friends and learning quite a bit. One night, I decided to go out and that is where it all began. I met a nice man, or so I was led to believe. He was working on the ferries from Felixstowe to Zeebrugge. He said, "Any time you want to go on the ship, I will be with you and make you welcome." This was great news and my friend agreed it was fantastic.

So, one weekend, I was off-duty, and my friend and I would go to see if it was true. We booked on the Viking Viscount, which was a Townsend Thoresen ship. We were made very welcome and introduced to the other crew too. I was very flattered by this man, and he made me feel good and I developed feelings for him. I decided that I had to see if he was really a nice man, as my friends had said to be careful. I was invited to a disco that night. We had a slow dance together and he was very polite and before he went back to work, he asked "Where are you from?" He also asked me if I was taken. He slipped me a note and kissed me on the cheek before his shift ended. I blushed and when he had gone, I read it with my friend. He had written his address and phone number and his name was Paul. He also added the date he would be off work on leave for two weeks, and he would love to meet up again. I took the note away with me as we disembarked from the ship. I made a note of the date, and I was looking forward to seeing him again, so we could get to know each other and take it from there.

As the days went by, I was getting nervous and excited. The day arrived and I was taken to meet his parents. His mum was a German national who had met his dad in England, who was a baker by trade. I was also introduced to his mum's boyfriend Terry, his sister Helga, and his brother George, who were visiting from Germany.

We all sat down and shared a meal; it was great. Terry asked me where I was staying, and I said sharing a flat with another trainee nurse. He offered to help me out as he owned several flats in Ipswich, and he would charge me very little rent. So, I said I would love to.

I went to my shared flat and told my flat mate, she asked with a worried look on her face "Are you sure you know what you are doing? This seems very fast." I simply said yes, and within the week, I moved into the new flat. It was a spacious one-bedroom flat overlooking the main road.

Life seemed good and everything was going well. I started living with Paul. I called my mum and gave her the address. I invited her over saying the next time she was off; I would like her to meet Paul and see what she makes of him. She was delighted and gave me the dates when she was next off.

Life was good and I was delighted with him and his family, they had made me so welcome. His mum told me more about her son, how he had been in a bad relationship, and she cheated on him, and she now has a child saying that it's Paul's. I said that he should take a DNA test to be sure. But nothing more was said about it. As the days went by, I was clearly falling in love with him. Mum came down as promised. I met her from the train in Ipswich and we hugged. As we travelled to the flat, she was asking me a lot of questions about Paul. When we arrived at the flat, mum slept on my bed settee.

The next day, I took her to meet the family, they made her very welcome, and we shared dinner together. Mum was delighted. After dinner, we went back to the flat and we sat and talked all night. She was quizzing me and wanted to know if he was the one. I simply smiled sweetly and blushed. Paul came round the next morning to meet mum, before his next shift on the ship. He was polite and mum was thrilled as he kissed her hand. As they were talking, I made a hot drink and he asked mum, "Could I please have your permission to marry Heather?" She wasn't very happy about this, I was only seventeen, and she thought it was too quick as we hadn't been going out for long. But he persuaded her saying that we really love each other.

She said, "Well, if that's the way you feel, then go ahead. I just hope it works out for you both." He said that the next time he was off we will get our rings.

Mum returned home and said that the next time she came, she would like to go on the Townsend Thoresen ship that Paul worked on to see how he is at work. After she had left, I said to Paul that we must go to Scotland to meet my family and friends.

He agreed and a week later, we went to Scotland, where he met my brother Jonas, his wife Leslie, Sheena and Chris and many more people who wanted to meet this stranger. Everyone was surprised to see me with a young man. They all said he was nice, but weird! I laughed "What do you mean? He has a strange laugh, and it makes him sound like a crazy person, but he is charming and kind." He was made welcome in both Dornoch and Embo. To all my relatives and friends, he told them we were getting married, and it would be a big wedding, and everyone was invited. Everyone was shocked and asked me if it was true, to which I blushed and said yes. They were all pleased for us.

We stayed for two weeks and visited mum working in the jail craft shop and restaurant. In between doing her baking in the pantry and serving customers, we shared tea, and she took Paul to see the tweeds they had made on the premises. We met my mum's friends in the weaving department, where he was made most welcome. He had planned to buy a kilt or a tartan skirt for his mum and he was surprised that everyone was friendly here. He bought some gifts for his family. Paul offered mum some money to get herself a dress and hat for the wedding. He said that next time we come up here, it would be for the wedding. Mum was visibly upset and when I asked her what the problem was. She frowned. "Heather Ann, this is all a bit sudden. Are you sure you aren't rushing things?"

She didn't want me to leave yet, but I said, "It won't be for long. And you can come and visit us whenever you like." She begrudgingly agreed and said that she would visit soon.

We headed back home to Ipswich and Paul was saying that his mum, dad, and stepdad were going to be helping with the wedding funding. We all got together, and after making plans, his parents went with us to Embo. They made an arch of flowers around the door as was the German custom. Everyone was stunned. After everything was almost ready, the day before the wedding, mum had made loads of cakes and sandwiches for all the invited guests. I decided to help mum with the teas and coffees. Just then, a man came through the door and Jonas my brother ran to him and shook his hand. I recognised him almost at once, he was Harold James Backhurst, the man I had known as dad for years.

I said, "Thank you for coming up, father, to see me before I get married, you'll be walking me down the aisle then."

"Good Heavens, no! I am not your father. I'm only here because my son Jonas had invited me," he exclaimed loudly, seeming quite alarmed.

I ran to the kitchen in tears and said to mum, "Harold just said he's not my father? He said that my father was dead or so he thinks." Mum became very quiet and red faced.

"Heather Ann, I am so sorry that you found out that way. I tried to hold it back from you because every time I talk about him, it hurts badly. You're the only good thing to come out of all this."

She hugged me tightly with tears flowing down her cheeks. As I went back into the room as mum told me to, Harold and Paul and his mum were busy arguing about the war. The guests were getting edgy and thinking of leaving until Mum came in shouting, "What the hell is going off in here?" Paul's mum Ina said it's him causing trouble.

Mum turned to Harold and said, "You, are always causing trouble, Harold. I thought you might have changed but it seems not. So, get out of my house and never come back."

He turned on his heels and with a curt goodbye, he left. Mum apologised for his behaviour, and everyone was dismissed. I went to bed with my eyes brimming with tears. What did he mean, my dad is dead? Who was he? I wished he was there instead of that horrible man.

The next day was my wedding day, I went to have breakfast and mum and I were around the breakfast table when I said sorry for what happened. She said kindly, "Don't be, it's not your fault." My brother Jonas was going to give me away and he was all suited and booted. He was needing Dutch courage and had one too many until he had to sit down.

I arrived at the top of the stairs and mum was gushing at me. She told me that I looked beautiful with the dress and the veil, and the bridesmaids looked great. She said, "This is the last time I will ask you, but are you sure you know what you are doing?"

"Yes, of course, I am sure, I love him, mum!" I replied.

"Good, that's all I need to hear as once you get married there is no way back." We hugged each other and I said I was ok, and that Paul's family was good to me.

Mum left with the bridesmaids, and I was left alone with Jonas waiting for the wedding car. He was quite tipsy and was laughing all the time. I was not happy with him. As the car arrived, he was outside throwing loose pennies and people were outside throwing rice over me. I thought it was weird but was told it was for good luck!

When I arrived at the church, I was led down the aisle with Jonas being rather unsteady to the altar. There was Paul waiting at the altar and he smiled, and I gave a nervous smile back. I was here to get married to this man, whom I thought was the love of my life. The service was lovely and afterwards, we were led to the reception and the dance. We danced the night away and then, suddenly, it was over, and Paul and I went to our room at the castle for the night, before we were due to head down south for our honeymoon.

The next day, we went to see mum before we headed south for our honeymoon. I was inside the house and heard giggling. I looked outside and there was Paul driving a bright yellow Robin Reliant, with people standing around giggling. They were all saying, 'it's the Yellow Submarine.' We both got in and it started, but it only got as far as the bus stop, then it packed in completely! What an embarrassment, I felt such a disgrace and couldn't show my face to anyone in Embo. It was the talk of the village. Mum was laughing and so were his parents. I hid my face with shame.

He called the AA. They arrived in an hour and loaded it on a trailer with 'Just Married' hung on it. We also had to travel with the vehicle as the driver could only go as far as the border and then we would have to change driver. The local newspaper took photos, and the driver brought me a bouquet and a nice card saying congratulations and have a safe journey from the AA. When we arrived at the border, the new driver loaded the three-wheeler on his trailer, and we left for Ipswich. This took many hours, and the car was taken to the garage, and we went home.

Paul asked me to go with him to Germany on his motorbike to meet more of his family. I was nervous having no knowledge of the German language. We went on the ferry. When got to the German border, we stopped at a café and the German Police were outside looking at the British motorbike. Paul went out and spoke with them and they were happy and left. Now, he had brought with us a bottle of whisky, but he hadn't tied it on properly and it fell and was smashed. He got very annoyed at me, but then said it wasn't my fault. After all, it was him who had put it on the back.

Finally, we arrived at his grandparent's house and met with the rest of the family. I was very nervous and shocked, as neither of his grandparents spoke any English. I was asked to go to the cellar and get a bottle of wine. I headed down to the basement. It was dark and musty, and I was scrabbling around for the light switch. I stopped open mouthed and there before me was a poster of Adolf Hitler with the words ' Hitler' and a massive swastika. I knew that this was something I was not meant to see, so I just grabbed a bottle of wine and headed upstairs. I was very scared and was longing for the UK. I found it very difficult trying to understand what they were all saying. I had to ask Paul at the time, what they were saying. I was so young and innocent and had no idea. We stayed there for a week and to me, it was a week of hell. I didn't understand what was going on. There were no mobiles in those days and the only phone was the house phone but that would be very expensive to use. I took Paul aside and said, "I'm not very comfortable or happy here. Could we please go home?"

The next day, we got ready to leave and after a few stifled farewells, we rode off. He didn't speak to me and on the ferry, I asked him what I had done. He said, "The sooner we get home the better, then I will talk to you." I became scared and very frightened of him for the first time ever. He said, "We shall have a family to bring us closer together." I agreed and decided to come off the pill. Sadly, nothing happened.

A few months later, Paul said we should invite mum down to say thank you for the wedding she prepared for us. He would pay for a trip on his ship, The Viking Viscount. Mum was delighted and was dreaming of her duty-free haul as she travelled down. Mum asked me how married life was treating me. I said he has his moments but we're happy.

She asked, "Has he hurt you?"

"No. We're planning on having a family. I'm off the pill now."

I even told her about Paul being accused of fathering another child. Mum said he should have a DNA test. But I told her that he was not going to as we argued about it. Mum said, "He is guilty, that's why he wants a child with you to say he is happily married and a family too." I just told her to leave it.

Mum and I went shopping the next day and I went into Mothercare dreaming of babies. I said to mum, "I would love to have a child, just think how happy I will be."

She said, "If God allows it, you will." We visited Paul's mum and dad and her boyfriend and his dad's sister. We enjoyed a tea of sandwiches and tea. Mum told Ina and Terry about the trip Paul had arranged for us. "Ooh, Lovely. You'll be able to get lots of duty-free to take back to Scotland. All you need is a day passport." Mum saw Sidney, Paul's dad, was in a separate room and asked Ina, "Why he is in there and you in here?" She said he likes it that way.

Mum went in with Sidney and talked about his situation. He told about how Terry was Ina's lodger and lover and wasn't afraid to flaunt it. He promised to tell mum all the story one day, when they were alone. As we prepared to leave, Ina said with a hint of venom in her voice, "Ignore him, whatever he says to you is all lies. He's just jealous."

The next day, I was at work and phoned mum to see if she was ok. She said that Sidney had invited her round as Ina and Terry had gone away for a bit. I said to her mind the crossings near the flat. You will have to press the button and only cross when you see the green man.

She laughed a deep laugh and said, "Heather, the only green men I see are the ones coming out of the Eagle Pub, drunk!"

So, I laughed with her and left her to it.

Mum visited Sidney and managed the crossings safely. They had tea and crumpets, and he was saying how he met Ina. He was in Germany with the army, and they met in a crowded bar. They became attached and decided to marry. When she came over here, she took up with the man who is the lodger, Terry.

"She didn't really want me," Sidney said sadly, "it was just a plan to get a passport out of Germany. I am a baker by trade, and this is my house. I am not leaving but if she wants to, she can."

"Terry owns property," he continued, "across Ipswich, and he's loaded. We have three children, Two boys and a daughter. Even now, I am saying she isn't mine, she's

Terry's." Mum was shocked and couldn't believe it. Mum and Sidney agreed to be friends and she would speak with him whenever he needed anything. He was delighted.

The next day, I was on a late shift, so we went to the centre to get our day passport to go on the Townsend Thoreson's Viking Viscount. We were booked on for the weekend and we couldn't wait. I knew Paul was working that weekend on the ship. He came home to see how we were getting on, then went straight back to the ship ready for the night's voyage.

We were just boarding the ship and we met the crew which I had already met when I met Paul. They were all very welcoming and they had set up a first-class dinner for mum and me. It was very posh, and Paul had thought of everything and there was a bucket with ice in it with a bottle of champagne. That must have cost him a lot of money. We drank about half of the bottle and gave the rest to the staff for their welcome.

We went to our lovely cabin, and we slept well. In the morning, we had breakfast served to our cabin and got ready to go to the duty-free shop. Mum's eyes nearly popped out. She had never seen so much for so little. She was shopping like a mad woman. She bought another bottle with a ship in it for a keepsake as she had lost the other one. She also bought flags for my brother Jonas and perfume for my brother's wife Leslie.

As we prepared to leave the ship, we were ushered through customs and we decided to go through the green, nothing to declare channel. Mum and I were called over to see the customs officer and he said to mum as she showed him her ship in a bottle.

"On a ship, off a ship and now you have a ship in a bottle, I don't get it. It must be a Scottish thing. I know there's one crew member who is your son-in-law, so we'll leave it there. But, if you go aboard again, be extra careful and try not to overload yourself or you may be caught out and have to pay more." Mum was puzzled but I explained it later.

We headed to our home and mum was very thankful for the trip; she remarked how kind and caring Paul was and so lovely. She gave him a hug and was full of praise for him. He smiled, "Anytime, have a safe journey home." We each had tears in our eyes and after we hugged, she was away.

After work the next day, which had been a good day, I went to visit my in-laws, and Ina took me to one side and gave me an ice pick.

I said, "What's that for?"

She said, "It's for protection. If anyone follows you and won't take no for an answer, stab him and then run home. He won't bother you again."

I took it and as I walked home, I sensed someone was following me and my hand gripped the pick. But soon I was home and breathed a huge sigh of relief. As Paul was working, I slept with the light on all night as I was scared.

As I was coming home from work, I saw one of our neighbours working on his car, he said, "You're Paul's wife?"

"Yes," I said.

"I'm Tim, I live in the flat above you and I work down the docks too. My wife Dawn also works for Townsend Thoresen in the office." They invited me over for a coffee to have a chat. How lovely to have friendly neighbours. The next day, I went in for a coffee and Dawn was on her own and we chatted for hours while the men were at work. She asked me if I was happy and I said of course, I am happily married. She said that's good, that's the best way to be. Dawn told me that her man had got her the job in the office. I said that I would love to work on the ships, but not the same one as Paul. Dawn smiled and we agreed to be good friends and we would always be there for each other.

The next day, it was like ships passing in the night, I was going to work, and Paul was coming home, so I left him a wee note and made dinner and went to work. As I returned home, Tim and Dawn knocked at the door and invited us both up for coffee and a couple of drinks. I had to not drink too much, as I was on a back shift. We had a great time and I told Tim how I wanted to work on the sister ship 'The Herald of Free Enterprise.' Tim and Paul said that I should write a letter asking if there is a job for you on the sister ship as there seemed to be a lot of work available.

Then Paul can take it to the office who will pass it to HR and the captain who would decide if I was suitable for the job. So that's what I did, and Dawn seemed very happy with it.

The next day, we were talking about work, and I walked into a lovely smell. Paul had made us dinner and I asked him if he had delivered the letter to the captain. He had and we had dinner and were having a few drinks. Paul said we should go and see his mum and her boyfriend, but I just wanted to rest and enjoy each other's company. He flew into a rage.

I said, "I don't like taking sides. I like your dad, but your mum wants me to ignore him. I just don't like ignoring people."

He really went for me. I was punched and kicked and slapped, he took the flat phone away from me and I had two black eyes. He punched me so many times in the stomach, I couldn't move. I went to my bed, and he called my work and told them I wasn't well. I really was not in a good way, I wanted to get back to my mum and wish I had never entered this relationship.

I said to him, "Why did you do this to me?"

He just looked at the floor and said sorry and we should forget it and move on. The doctor came out and asked me what happened. So, after I had told him, he threatened Paul and said if it happens one more time, he will be reported to the police. He said to the doctor it wouldn't happen again.

Mum came down to see me for a few days as Paul had gone back to work on the ship. She was horrified at how I looked, and she said, "Thank goodness, you don't have a family." She couldn't understand how he was so nice to her yet, now here he was showing his true colours.

A few days later after mum had gone home, I was due to meet him and his friends. They were all coming into town to get some snacks. I saw his friend Phillip first, who said, "Why are you wearing sunglasses when it's not sunny? Take them off."

I said, "No!"

He said, "Come on, I just want to see your bonny face."

As I removed the glasses, I said, "Well, do you think that's bonny?"

His face fell and he looked completely stunned.

"Who the hell did that to you?"

I told him that Paul had done this to me. He said, "Where is he the little eejit?"

I said, "I think he's working or up at his mam's."

"Why on Earth did he do this to you?"

I said that it was because I didn't want to go to his mams every day.

He said, "It was a damn shame doing this to such a bonny girl. He should never have done this to you, does he think he can control you? You need to have a life of your own and he should never hit a woman. That's just wrong. You know if he tried it with the guys on the ship, they would tell him to take a running jump! You leave it to me, and we'll see if he is a real man when I tell the lads what he did to your face. See if he owns up to what he did to you, then we'll see what the boys have to say about it."

I just smiled a weak smile and said. "Please don't hurt him, just give him a good talking-to."

Over the next few days, Paul was away with the ship and mum came down for a holiday. She was visiting her friends in Felixstowe. As she was getting ready and we were having a coffee, we heard the front door go with a loud bang. Paul staggered through the door holding his ribs and bleeding from his lips and a matching set of black eyes. I asked him, "Who did this to you?"

He said, "You f***ing well know who did this to me, B***h! I want you out of my life altogether!" Mum and I went upstairs to the friends in their flat and Dawn came out on the landing. "What the hell is going off?"

She had heard the shouting and came out to see. We were ushered into her flat and she asked me, "Are you ok?" I told her what Paul had done to me and the guys at the docks had heard about it and he got his comeuppance from the guys as they didn't like wife beaters. He looked like he had a few broken ribs, a pair of black eyes and a broken nose. She said, "I know the crew don't like women beaters. You should go back to Scotland where you will be safer away from his beatings and his mum and her dodgy lodger. If he loves you as he says he does, he will stand up to his mum and tell her he lost it with you, and this is what he got for beating you up. The boys on the docks really don't like women beaters."

I got my stuff and went with mum to see her friends and stay for a few days. I went to see a solicitor and we had a good chat and he said I should file for a divorce. I told him everything about what had happened, and he said,

"That's not on. You would be safer and better off out of it. It sounds like he has a split personality. He may even kill you and not know he has done it."

He then suggested that I take time out and return to Scotland and stay there until the divorce is finalised. But first I would need to take out an injunction on him to prevent him coming anywhere near me. So, I agreed and signed the appropriate papers.

But, before I could leave, I had to go and see my work colleagues and my bosses. After I had told them, I had to give a month's notice to leave, and they were very understanding. I also went to talk to Ina, Paul's mum; Terry, the lodger and Sidney, his father. They said they were sorry it wasn't working out and Ina asked if I had thought of going to marriage guidance counselling. I told them I had taken legal advice from my solicitor, and they were quite upset, although Sidney winked at me with a grin and said he was right behind me. Ina said, "He can change, it's just a temper he's got!"

I said, "No! It's more than that: he has a split personality."

She got really upset at this.

As I was leaving, I saw Paul pull up out the back of the house with his motorbike. He saw me and was calling me all kinds of nasty names. So, I just put my head down, eyes filled with tears and stormed out the house heading home. I really needed to be on my own and all the while what had happened was returning to my memory. At first, I thought he was lovely, but little did I know what he was capable of.

I was walking down the main street in Ipswich, still sniffling, and feeling rather low. I looked both ways and as there was nothing coming, I crossed the road, but I never reached the other side. I was hit by a fast motorbike and knocked high into the air; my shoes ended up in someone's garden. My broken body lay strewn across the road. I was told the motorbike stopped and looked back, but then rode off at speed. A lovely lady stayed with me as somebody phoned an ambulance. I hadn't a clue what had happened.

"You've been in an accident, love. Some mad people on a motorbike ran you over at great speed. It was difficult to see who it was, but you took the full force of the collision."

There was blood coming out of my ears and as the ambulance appeared the police were there too. I was put on a stretcher and my head was placed in a collar and head guard. The lady wished me well and said take care. My shoes were also put on the stretcher. The police were busy asking questions and I was rushed off to hospital. After the first tests, I was told I was very lucky, I only had concussion and I had very bad bruising on my back. They were all shocked at how little I had suffered. Someone must be looking after you, the nurse said, as she put me into a taxi to take me home. I was in for most of the day until they said I was fine to go home with a walking stick.

Mum was waiting for me when I got home. She was very shocked to see me the way I was.

"For God's sake, I wish you had never married him!"

I asked, "How do you know it's him? It could have been anyone."

"Well," she said, "how come it's started now and never before? In all my days I had looked after you and never had much trouble, but that was until you had your head turned." Paul turned up at the flat and was very quiet. Mum said to him, "Did you knock my daughter down by any chance?"

He said, "Yes, I did it to make her see sense, but I am sorry, it was bad of me to do that to you. It was just a laugh!"

I stood up and said it was not a laughing matter, this was serious, and he could have killed me.

"Why did you do it?" He said, "I wanted you to see sense and not get legal advice about ending the marriage."

I was raging and said, "We are done! I do not want you anymore."

I had already packed his bags and he yelled back at me, "…Then go and never come back or come near me ever again!"

I said, "I am going to file for a divorce and move back to Scotland." He went quiet again and I believe he understood it was the end.

The next day, I went to see the solicitor and told him to go ahead for the divorce and also an injunction to stop him coming anywhere near me. I told him that Paul had also run me over and why he said he had done it.

The solicitor said, "Ok. The judge will have a field day with him and so will I."

He wrote everything down and the injunction was in place after two days.

I took mum to the train station to see her off and told her that I would be in touch about returning home and the solicitor had arranged an injunction so that as soon as the ship returned to port, he would be served the injunction notice. If he went against it, he would be arrested and put in jail.

Mum said that she will get Jonas to hire a van when I am ready to help me get my stuff back home to Scotland. I agreed to this and when everything was settled, I would be returning home. She also reminded me that I had nice friends in the block who would look after me until that time.

Chapter 7
A Fresh Start with a Fixed Heart!

Professor Terrence English

After a few weeks, I was due to return to Scotland. First, I had to return to work to hand my uniform in. I met with the matron and gave her a potted plant and chocolates to say thank you. She said that she was sad to see me go, but she understood that I couldn't live with a man with a split personality. She said that she would be willing to give me a reference anytime I needed one as I was a good worker. I rose to head for the door, and I collapsed. The doctor was called for. The doctor looked very ashen faced and demanded an ambulance be called for right away. I was transferred to the local A&E, and they decided to transfer me to Papworth Hospital under the care of the eminent heart surgeon Professor Terrence English. I was taken into a side room and Professor English came in to see me and after reading my chart he looked at me and smiled.

"So, my dear, what brings you here to me?"

I was telling him about my heart problems from a young age and that I collapsed in Ipswich, and they said it was my heart and they were sending me here to you. He looked at the tablets I showed him and threw them in the bin.

"What kind of doctors do you have in Scotland? These tablets are useless, do they not care? They can't be doing their jobs right. A right bunch of lazy nutters you have up there. I suggest that you get in touch with your family as I have some bad news." I phoned mum and said that the doctor needs to talk to you right away. The doctor had mum on loudspeaker and said that I only had a few days to live, and I would need emergency heart surgery. I was shocked and began to cry, but Mr English said, "Shush, child, I will do my best to keep you alive!"

Mum was in shock on the phone, and she hung up with a sniffle.

Back in Embo, mum was frantically trying to get in touch with people to arrange to leave to come to Papworth Hospital in Cambridgeshire. It was a long way and there would be many hours of prayer and fretting. How would she cope? But she trusted in her Lord Jesus. I phoned mum later and she answered sounding flustered.

"I am in the big Papworth Hospital where they do heart operations."

She said, "Don't you be worrying, Heather Ann, I know where you are. Jonas will look after everything here and I will talk to my boss, and I will be leaving very soon. Everyone here is praying for you and they have all chipped in for the rail fare." I was shocked and began to be teary.

She said, "Now, now, my girl, everything will be well. I will see you tomorrow."

The very next day, I heard that mum had caught the sleeper train from Inverness that night and had travelled all the way down and arrived in the morning. She said that she had had no sleep and was just sat there praying all the time. She must have dropped off, however, as she awoke with a jolt near Crewe. She shook herself and was wide awake for the change at London. She turned up at the front door and came in and was taken to my bedside. When she saw me, she gasped and began to cry and hugged me tighter than ever before.

"Oh, my girl, I am sorry for you!"

"I am fine, mum. Don't you be worried about me. I'll be fine."

I was very surprised that she got there that fast. I asked her if she had got everything sorted at home.

"Yes, don't you worry about anything, everything is covered by the grace of God."

Mr English came in and shook mum's hand and they had a wee chat. He said that I was very lucky to be here and that he was going to perform a new style of operation to repair my heart. I would be the first woman in this operation. "I will be operating through the back as she is such a young lady. We don't want an unsightly scar now to do we? I will try my best

114

to save her life. She will be in ICU for at least a week and then it depends on her body, how it reacts to the operation. I hope you can stay here as it's going to take quite some time." He explained thoroughly.

"I am ok with that, sir, thank you. My son is taking care of everything at home," mum said. They offered mum a room at the hospital, so she wouldn't have to pay for anywhere. I also spoke to Mr English and told him about my ex Paul and how he wanted to destroy me and kill me.

He reassuringly said, "Don't you worry about that; the security guards know how to deal with that type of thing and as your mum is here nobody else matters. Relax and try not to worry. Everything will be fine, you'll see."

As mum was having a meal in the restaurant, she met a lady from Bellshill in Glasgow and was amazed that she was not the only parent from Scotland there. Her son was having a heart transplant, he was doing quite well in the ICU. Mum felt encouraged that she was not alone going through this. She returned and told me that she had made a friend. I was pleased that she had someone to talk to. Then the trolley came for me. I was very scared and looked to my mum for support.

I hugged mum and said, "See you soon."

She said, "Cheerio for now. I'll see you later in the ICU."
-0oOo0-

That later turned into a week!

I opened my eyes for the first time, and it was like an abattoir. There were men all crying out in pain with blood on the floor and machines flashing and beeping and blood transfusions bags everywhere. I drifted back to sleep and what seemed like an age later, I opened my eyes fully and turned to my left and there was a young man getting a visit from a lady

I thought was his mam. She looked happy that he was awake and talking to her. I then felt a touch on my right hand and there was the smiling face of my mum. I asked her had I only been sleeping for a day?

She said, "No, sweetheart, you have been out for a week!"

"A week?" I said, "It didn't feel like it."

"I know, sweetheart. But you're alive and back with us again. You don't need to worry about anything, your brother is taking care of everything in Scotland."

Mum tried to move her chair slightly and the alarm on the monitor went off into a steady noise. Mum went pale and began to panic. The nurse came over and told her not to panic, it's just resetting. She thought that I had died. I was concerned for mum and asked her how can she do all this for me? She said, "You are a gift from God, and I trust your care to Lord Jesus."

Mum had formed a close friendship with the lady from Bellshill. They were very supportive of each other, and they both were believers, and their faith bolstered their strength. Two doctors came to help me get out of ICU.

They said, "We need to take that from you, first!"

By that they meant the blood drain tube in my side.

"What's that for?" I questioned.

"It's drained the old bad blood away from your wound."

These doctors gave me a local anaesthetic and called the surgeon over. So, while the two doctors held me down, the surgeon gently started pulling the tube out of my side. I was screaming loudly as the pain was very severe. One more tug and the tube was out, and the relief was instant. They put a couple of stitches into the wound, and I was cleaned up. They transferred me from ICU into the ward where Mum was waiting for me.

As we were chatting, Mr English came over to see me and asked how I was feeling now the tube was out I smiled and said, "Fine, thank you."

Jokingly, he turned to my mum and said, "I can do you next if you wish. I have a few spaces now!" She smiled "You've got no chance!" He grinned and sniggered then walked away chuckling.

Mum was chatting to the staff nurse who was checking my stitches and she asked her what she could get for Mr English to thank him for saving my life. She smiled and said he wouldn't accept any gifts. But mum insisted, and she asked, "whisky or chocolates?" So, after the staff nurse left, mum turned to me and said, "Right, that's settled then. I'll get two gifts, chocolates for the nurses and whisky for the main man himself."

I said, "You'll get shot for that!"

"Who cares," she said, "you're my only daughter and they have done a fantastic thing in saving your life!"

Mum went away and returned shortly with the two gifts. She delivered a huge box of chocolates to the nursing station, and they were blushing, smiling and trying to refuse the gift, as it was their job. But mum would have none of their refusals and they eventually just gave in and said thank you.

Then she went to find Mr English in his office and presented him with the litre bottle of whisky, he tried to refuse but mum was insistent, and he accepted and offered her a wee dram too. She thanked him for saving my life. He replied, "It was a pleasure, as if I hadn't operated then she would not be here. All the doctors in Scotland would only give her pills. I have written them a letter too blasting their inadequacies and just allowing their patients to continue suffering until their untimely deaths. It's a good job that she was here." Mum agreed and they clinked glasses and she toasted "Sláinte!" which means, 'To your health.'

Mum returned to my bedside and kissed me on the cheek.

"Now then, my girl, I will go to your flat and pack you some clothes and things you will need as you're coming home to Scotland to convalesce. I will have a word with my boss to give me my holidays now, as I have saved a lot of them for you."

I said, "I hope I will not be too much of a handful." She replied, "You are my only daughter, and I would always look after you. By the grace of God, we'll get through this."

The following Friday, they had agreed that I would be allowed home to convalesce. But, before they would let me go, Mr English came to examine my scar and he smiled and indicated that the stitching was a good job.

I smiled through teary eyes and said, "Thank you for saving my life. I don't know what I would have done if you hadn't saved my life."

He said, "You're most welcome, young lady, now go and have a good life and remember to show off your scar and tell everyone how lucky you were to have your life. Take care and God bless."

I said to mum I would probably be pushing up the daisies if I hadn't been working down here. She said, "God must have put you here to save your life." They brought my tablets and my letter for the Scottish doctors, and we were in the waiting room waiting for the taxi to take us to the train station. Mum looked around and saw her friend from Bellshill, they exchanged addresses and she said she was still waiting for the results after her son's operation. We gave our goodbyes and she said directly to me, "You have a lovely mum who is a lovely friend, a Godsend. Take care."

The train journey back to Scotland was a long tiresome journey, but I was relieved that I was alive and going home to be with my family, away from my bad marriage and everything. We got home to be greeted by most of the village. They were smiling and saying how pleased they were that I was alive, and the surgeon saved my life. I thanked them all for their prayers and went inside to relax after our long journey.

Mum and her friend from the hospital had been writing each other for a couple of weeks and things were going well.

But one day, mum received a letter, and she sat down with a sigh.

I said, "What's up, Mum?"

Mum looked at me with tears in her eyes. She said, "Can you remember that lady who was at Papworth with her son? Well, he has died, I'm sorry to say." Tears fell like rain. She went on, "The new heart he was given was rejected by his body. He was fine for a while, but then one day, it stopped."

Mum and I just held each other and cried. In the letter, she thanked mum for being her friend and she wished us all the best for the future. But mum said that she would continue writing.

A few weeks later, mum was still looking after me and the council were asked if they could help us get a more suitable house as my stuff was filling hers. We were told to wait a few weeks.

During this time, a strange thing was happening. Throughout the night and over a few weeks, we were getting strange phone calls. These were silent calls with heavy breathing. We contacted the police, and they said keep a note of the calls what was said and times and dates. One day, the police were at the house and took a recording and the call was traced back to Bradford Road in Ipswich and the local police were informed and he was arrested and fined and ordered to stop. Mum changed her number, and all was quiet again.

Over the next few weeks, I got stronger and stronger. I received a letter from my barrister in Ipswich, calling me down to the court for the divorce case. I asked Jonas if he could hire a van to help me move my stuff up to Scotland at the same time.

The four of us travelled down to Ipswich in the van. It was a long hard journey, but we managed to arrive in time for court. I was dropped off at the court while the others went to get my stuff and I said I would be there after the court.

As I got into the court building, I was ushered into a side room to wait for my solicitor. I was surprised to see that Paul was called into the court room and I was left outside. I waited for ages and then my barrister came into the room and explained, "The divorce has been agreed without the need to speak with you. The police records and witness statements had decided the issue. He showed unreasonable behaviour and split personality."

I thanked the barrister and he said, "Have you got any plans for the future?" I said that my family were here with me, and I was moving back home to Scotland. He wished me all the best and left the room. I walked out of the room and glimpsed Ina out of the corner of my eye and as I stepped outside, I breathed a huge sigh of relief and went to be with the rest of the family. We emptied the flat and left his stuff and I said my goodbyes to Dawn upstairs and then we left. We travelled through the night and finally arrived in the morning back in Sutherland. I was tired, but glad to be home. I would miss my good friends from Ipswich but am much safer here in Scotland.

I applied for a nursing job at Cambusavie Hospital in Golspie. I was amazed that they decided to take me on. I had a fantastic boss in that hospital. I was given lovely accommodation in Bonar Bridge. This was close enough to my mum's for visits. Things were finally going well for both mum and me.

Mum had planned a weekend to see family in Inverness. Donnie and Jean were called my uncle and auntie but were not real blood relatives. They owned a guest house. We went down with my friend Dana, and we were told to go for a night out with Uncle Donnie. He would keep us safe as we don't know Inverness. We managed to dodge Donnie and went to another pub. Here we met two nice guys who were looking for a good night out.

These guys bought us both a drink. I thought I knew one of the men from school as he went out with a girl who couldn't handle distance relationships. His name was Jacob, and a part of his work was away for six months of the year delivering perfume from ports abroad. His friend Irwin was in the army and away from home.

We were chatting away, and he gave me his address, which was up on the West Coast and Irwin his friend was living in Bettyhill. We decided to stroll up to the castle and sit on the benches and continue talking. Jacob said that he was in school with me, but a year under me. He was in training in the Merchant Navy training to be an officer on the ship and then captain in charge of his own ship. I told him that I was nursing in Bonar Bridge, at which he said that he passes the road regularly and might see me!

We became pen pals and wrote to each other regularly until he was next on leave. I told mum.

She said, "Oh, no! Not another one on a ship. I thought you had enough of the first one that worked at sea."

I said, "This guy is training to be an officer and on to captain. His family stay on the West Coast and are Christians too. They're not Germans this time either."

Our writing to each continued while he was away on the ship across the world. Once he was back at home, I had a weekend off from my job in Bonar Bridge and he came to visit Dornoch, and I took him to meet my mum. He brought her a bunch of flowers and was very nice to her. They got talking about my first marriage to an Englishman with German ancestry. He used to beat Heather and even tried to kill her. My new Merchant Navy officer was shocked. He hated bullies. He would never do that to me! Mum was pleased to hear that, but still unsure. We shared a meal together.

He then went back to the West Coast to see his parents and we were meeting each other every now and again. We were getting on well and I was really liking him. He was nothing like Paul. He returned to sea for another very long time. I was working away in the hospital and continued writing every day to each other. I was also starting knitting jumpers for him to keep myself busy. When he returned home, he was overjoyed to receive them.

Sadly though, I lost a lot of friends when I was with him. He became very jealous and didn't like me mixing with anyone in case, they lead me astray. I became like a lonely old maid all alone until he returned home on leave and his friend too was on leave from the army at the same time.

We all had a good time, and Irwin was telling me all about Jacob. He told me how jealous he gets if anyone chats to his woman. Irwin said he didn't need to be as I am a one-man woman. He should trust me. Irwin bought me a bunch of flowers and Jacob bought me a bottle of perfume from his destination off the ship. I had never had anyone buy me perfume before. I was quickly falling for him. Mum too thought he was a lovely guy. Jacob invited me to go to him at his college before he returns to sea and stay with him for a few days. After our conversation, he left for his mum's, after we made a date for a couple of weeks' time.

I went to London on the train, and I was excited to see him again and looking forward to meeting his friends and seeing where he stayed. As we arrived at his digs, I found out that I was not really supposed to be there as it's for students only and I was not happy about it. He was not bothered as he said, "We'll be together forever!"

My heart leapt with joy.

"Really!"

He smiled and said, "Yes. I was planning on getting engaged to you and after two years married, if that's ok with you. After the two years, I will be an officer in the Merchant Navy."

We enjoyed our time together although when he was in college, I was lonely. Some of the other students weren't happy, but they let him off. We reminisced about school and who his first girlfriend was and what his interests were. Then the week was done.

He said he was staying in the college flat as he would be back on board the following week. He added that he would be away for a few months.

He pecked me on the cheek, and I boarded the train once more for home. It was a long journey, but I was daydreaming about him coming home and for me to be engaged and married again. My head was well and truly turned. When I returned home, mum was keen to know how it went, and I told her everything that happened especially the accommodation and she said,

"Why didn't he tell you that? You even took time off work too!"

I was in love, I didn't care. I also told mum; we were going to get engaged too. Mum smiled an uneasy smile and said, "Only if you're sure? Engaged is ok, but when you're married, you will be committed in the eyes of the Lord."

I went back to work and got the third degree there too. But I was in love. He came over regularly when he was on shore, and he visited my workplace and everyone there liked him and saw him as a polite young man. My friends in Dornoch were saying he was a nice guy, better than the last one. We were also visiting his parents at odd weekends. We got to know each other well. They were a Christian family and were regular churchgoers. Mum was overjoyed, as she attended the Free Church like the other family.

A few months later, we were planning to get engaged. But my brother said the same as my mum, make sure this is the right one, especially after what happened last time. I was blinded by love, and he was very charming and loved spending time together. He went back to college to finish his course. We were still writing every day and looking forward to getting together again.

When Jacob went back to the college, mum took me aside and spoke. "When you and Jacob are engaged, Heather, how would you like to have my old house in Embo? It will need stuff doing to it, but you can get a grant to do it up. It's too much for me to keep running it as I'm now based here in Dornoch."

I was surprised with this offer, but what about Jonas? Won't he need it? He already has a family.

She said, "Heather, my daughter, you have helped me so much and even when I was struggling. Your brother has his own house. I would love you to have it. It was built by your grandfather by his own hands. It's a family home for you and Jacob to live in."

I told mum that I would talk to him about it. She smiled and said thank you.

I spoke to Jacob about it, but he just started shouting about it.

"Why would I want to stay in Embo? It's a small village, we will be better off in a bigger village." I foolishly listened to him, and mum was very sad.

I said, "I'm only young and don't need property around my neck." I really upset her and then she decided to offer it to Jonas. He was very angry and annoyed. He said, "No! If you had offered it to me first then maybe, but because you offered it to Heather Ann first, no, just put it on the market!"

A few weeks later, I ended up in hospital. I didn't know what was wrong, until they told me that I was overdoing the pill. I had been taking it every day instead of stopping for my periods. The doctors were putting me straight as I was scared to get pregnant. While I was in hospital, I suffered a slight stroke, and my mouth went a funny shape, and I couldn't speak for a while. The staff looked after me and my mouth eventually went back to normal. When I was discharged, I went to stay with my mum to allow my body to rest.

Jacob was ready to ask me for my hand in marriage and he asked his parents and they said, "It's not us you need to ask. Its Heather's mum." So, he came over to see me and mum and bought her a bunch of flowers too. He asked her if he could marry me.

Mum said, "She is old enough now to make her own mind up, but you had better treat her right, after the man she was married to before."

He said he would never do anything like that to me. That weekend we got engaged and things were going well. Jacob even gave up training for his officer's position and went onto the long ships which delivered perfume to the UK. Then he was home monthly instead of the six months away. Every time he returned home, he always brought me perfume.

At New Year, I was invited to go to Liverpool and spend some time with him and the other girlfriends of the guys, as a special time off was agreed with the captain. All the ladies were swapping addresses to keep in touch so that we never feel alone when the guys are away. The weekend was fantastic and on the last day, we all were out drinking.

I fell out with him big time, because he drank too much and was staggering. I stormed off towards the ship with the other ladies and accidentally stepped on some sharp wire sticking up out of the pavement. It pierced my big toe and it bled fiercely. I had to get an injection into the bone and a painkiller and was told to rest it up. The captain was asked to not sail until a further day, as I wouldn't be fit enough. The guys were all moaning and groaning, as they were all told they would not get paid for the extra day, because they weren't working. Jacob was not popular. My toe and the rest of my foot felt better the next day and I returned home. I was glad to be home; I told mum about it and how they lost wages because of me, and Jacob wasn't popular with the crew.

I received a message from the ship Jacob was on and he was coming home on leave for a month. He was upset as he was too far away and wanted to be working near to me. This made me happier. He even went to my brother Jonas and asked him if there were any jobs going on the rigs. Jonas said there were jobs going on the rigs and the ships going out to them and delivering the rigging. At that time, the council offered me a council house which suited both of us. Everything was falling into place.

Chapter 8
For Better or for Worse?

Life was fine and we were seeing each other regularly; the wedding was decided upon, and mum called us in to see her. She turned to Jacob and said, "I will sell two of my caravans to pay for your wedding and part of your honeymoon."

I said, "You can't do that." Mum insisted so we happily agreed. Mum said it was our big wedding present from her. She booked the Burghfield Hotel in Dornoch and rooms for the West Coast families and the wedding party. My dress and the bridesmaid's dresses were bought and altered. Everything was almost ready. The Free Church of Scotland minister Reverend Macpherson came to see us both to discuss the wedding. We had to promise to attend church every Sunday for about six weeks before and after the wedding.

Wedding cars were prepared and polished, and the day of the wedding arrived. The guests, many of whom, I didn't know, were, arriving in Dornoch. I was getting ready in mum's house in Dornoch. Jonas was, once again, giving me away. He said, "I hope this is the last time, he seems like a nice guy."

I nodded and said, "Yes, it is the last time."

Nearer the time, mum came in and gave me a hug and said, "See you there." The bridesmaids, Moira and Juliet were looking very nervous, as they hadn't done this before. We all shared a drink and began to calm down in preparation for the day.

The car came to take me round to the church and as we arrived outside William the piper was walking in front of the car and we met Jemma, my niece, the flower girl. The day was very sunny, we returned to the Burghfield for the reception and the band was from the West Coast. Everyone enjoyed themselves, great food, great company, and plenty of drinks too! The photographer was a happy snapper taking plenty of pictures, and we all had had a great day.

At the end of the night, we went to our room and after I used the bathroom, I came out to ask Jacob to help me out of my wedding dress, but he was crashed out on the bed!

I felt so alone. Such a great start to married life. Could this be a sign of things to come? I went to the reception desk and asked the manager if he could help me to undo the clips as my new husband was crashed out on the bed and I can't do it myself. He followed me to the room and laughed at Jacob drooling on the bed.

He helped me and said, "What kind of a husband is he? If you were my wife, I would be the one looking after you. Not like this." He then turned and left.

In the morning, we had breakfast and left the hotel to get the bus to Inverness, then to change for the bus for Glasgow. As we arrived at the bus station, I was feeling a bit sickly and excused myself and went to the ladies. There was a lady in there and she asked me if I was ok. She gave me an anti-sickness pill and said you should be fine now.

I said, "I am on my honeymoon and don't want to be sick."

She said, "You will be fine now, my dear. Good luck on your honeymoon."

I felt so much better and went out to go to Jacob as we waited in the queue to get on the Glasgow bus, he asked me why I had taken so long in the toilets?

I said, "I met a lady who helped me when I was sick. She wished us luck on our honeymoon."

He smirked and said, "Funny that, I thought you had fallen in! Ha Ha!"

The journey to Glasgow wasn't too long and we were soon settling into our hotel. We rested until the evening mealtime approached. We went to the dining room for a few drinks. The waiter appeared at our table and took our order. Jacob gave me a look of seriousness. He said, "Now we are married; we should be very truthful with each other." I nodded. I always am.

He said, "Please don't be mad with me when I tell you something."

I said, "Go on then tell me what's on your mind."

He looked down and continued, "When I was looking after my mam's house in Glasgow, after she had died, we were cleaning the stuff out of her house, I will be honest with you. I had a few good drinks, and I was so depressed, and her next-door neighbour was there comforting me after my mams death. She was helping me out with getting rid of all her stuff. One thing led to another, and it happened. It wasn't meant to happen, but it did."

I was totally gobsmacked and shocked, we were engaged then. I didn't know what to do. He had even taken communion and promised he would be faithful. All I wanted to do was run away!

The meal was brought to us, and we ate in stony silence. I was not going to starve because my husband had been unfaithful. Jacob paid the bill, and I took the room key from him and went to the room alone. He stayed in the restaurant and did what he did best, he had quite a few more drinks. When he eventually came to the room, he wanted to argue about it, and he didn't see anything wrong as we weren't married then. But I fought back, and one thing led to another, and I ended up with two black eyes.

I feared him after that. In the morning, he was very apologetic. He even wondered why I had two black eyes.

I said, "We are going home," I wanted to be away from him, but there was nowhere else to go. I ended up buying a pair of sunglasses to hide the bruising. It was like eye shadow all over my eyes. I called mum to say that we were coming home, with the excuse that it was too expensive to stay all the time. One night was enough.

The next few hours heading home on the bus were a very silent affair. He couldn't even look at me. I just wondered what I had done wrong. As the bus arrived in Dornoch, my friends who were at the wedding saw us get off the bus and came over and asked me why I had sunglasses on as it wasn't sunny? I made an excuse that my eyes were just sore in the light. They just nodded and laughed, and we went on to my mum's house. As we entered, I ran straight upstairs to my room. Mum was shocked and asked Jacob.

"Why has she got sunglasses on, it's not sunny?" He just said that I had too much to drink, and her eyes are bloodshot.

Mum's friend Irene said, "I will go and see to Heather and see what I can do to help."

Now, Irene was an ex-cop and as soon as she saw me, she said, "Oh, my goodness, now I have seen it all. I could have him arrested for doing that!"

I said, "Please don't, I don't want to bring shame on the family! I have just got married for the second time. I love him, he didn't mean to do it!"

She said to me that if she ever saw this again, she would not hesitate to place the call and have him arrested. Men should never hit a woman. I said it's all to do with drink and saying he wants honesty after our wedding.

Things then began to settle down and both Jacob and I resumed our normal jobs. One day, I remember quite clearly sent shivers down my spine. That day was 6 March 1987. I was visiting my mum and was helping her make the evening supper, when I was busy in the kitchen and mum let out a yelping cry. I called through to her, "Are you ok, Mum?"

No response only sobbing. I called out again. This time mum said, "Oh, Heather Ann, you must come and see this." I came through after drying my hands and stopped dead in my tracks, tears began to trickle down my cheek. The Herald of Free Enterprise, the ship which I had applied to join had capsized and many friends of my ex-husband were feared dead. I had built up friendships with some of the crew who were posted on the ship. My heart sank and mum and I wept. She said that could have been you too on the ship. I phoned my friends in England and asked some questions; some were still officially missing. I couldn't believe it.

Herald of free Enterprise

Friends I had known for a few years suddenly, I would never see again, even some of the Norwegian boiler men, never made it. A few weeks later when the death toll number came out at 193, I was just stunned. As most people across the world were. I wept for my lost friends, but mum said, "Somebody must be looking after you up there."

To this day, I still remember the friendships I had built up and those poor friends who we lost on that fateful day.

I remember the first day we went on the sister ship, The Viking Voyager and met the crew quite a few of whom were on the Herald that day. I still cry when I remember, and I don't think I will ever forget. How could life continue as normal? So many people lost in the tragedy.

After some time of living, we finally moved into the council accommodation, and we were slowly settling down. I was incredibly happy and had made it a beautiful home.

I missed the pill and fell pregnant. Both families were overjoyed. One night, Scotland was playing England at football. I went into labour. Jacob was watching the match with our neighbour each going at the drink. They were matching each other drink for drink. His name was Jacob too. I was alone in the labour suite, and I gave birth to a beautiful baby girl. I phoned the neighbour, and they went to the pub and told him; he was overjoyed and even more so as Scotland had beaten England into the bargain. The baby's head was well and truly wetted. We went to see both sets of grandparents and everyone was incredibly happy for us and wished us well. We finally named her Tanya. Life was smooth again!

A few months later, we decided to decorate the spare room and create a nursery for Tanya. Everything was all done up lovely with the crib and changing tables and toys, teddies, and the like. We moved Tanya into the freshly decorated room. We had our own bedroom back for just the two of us.

The next day, our neighbour Jacob knocked for my husband, to go with him to play golf. They were also going to have a few drinks as well to celebrate our daughter's birth. Everything was running smoothly, and I had just got the dinner organised and as time went by, I was getting annoyed, he knew I was preparing his dinner. He eventually turned up home extremely late and his dinner was ruined, and I had a go at him. He gave me a mouthful of abuse and I walked away to get Tanya to feed her. He stormed upstairs and there was a great deal of banging and smashing. I just left him to it. *I'm not going to talk to him or even tackle him while he is in that mood, or he might turn on me!* Then the front door slammed, and he was away staggering side to side.

I gingerly walked up the stairs and oh my Gosh! He had totally trashed the nursery, it had all been thrown around and some bits smashed in his temper. Then the phone rang, and it was mum asking me if we needed a babysitter anytime, she would come over and help. I sniffed and she said, "Why are you crying, my child? Has he hurt you?"

"No, but the nursery is destroyed."

She said, "What do you mean destroyed? I'm coming over to see for myself." Upon her arrival, mum was very shocked and looked incredibly upset and was tearful.

"This needs to stop or one day, he might hurt you or the baby. He should pack up his drinking or it's going to destroy you both."

The next day, when he awoke, he saw what he had done and was mortified. He swore that it would never happen again. To me he was a man with two faces, the 'demon' drink, and the sober kind man. After that event it seemed things had calmed down.

Later after he had calmed down, he returned home to find both of us waiting for him. Mum launched off at him saying how stressful this is for me. I left them talking for about an hour, I went to bed with Tanya's crib next to me. He went to the spare room and began fixing things that he had broken. He also cleared away all the debris. This took him a few hours at least. When he came to bed finally, I must have dropped off to sleep.

As the months passed and Tanya was growing, we began to discuss having another baby, as company for Tanya to grow up with. As his drinking had calmed down then, we tried again, and I fell pregnant once more. Nine months later, I gave birth to a beautiful baby boy; we were delighted. Everything in the pregnancy was going well. We decided to name him George.

However, at the age of eight months, we took George for his first injections, (the 6 in 1, as it was known, Diphtheria, Hepatitis B, Polio, Tetanus and Whooping cough); this is where the problems started. George was rushed to hospital with a rash, he was having fits and was being sick. As I had to stay with him, because of his youthful age, mum offered to look after Tanya, while I was away. I stayed in the same room as George, who was attended by the nurses round the clock. It seemed never-ending, until the doctors called me into a side room for a wee chat. They told me they were doing tests and they had decided he was suffering from 'bowing fits,' which made his hands and feet shake and he would pull his head down. They also said that he was a bit afraid of the light as they tried to shine a torch into his eyes. They returned after a short while with another report and said that he has meningitis. That's why he was afraid of the light. That accompanied by the whooping cough vaccine triggered it. That's why he has the fits, and he should never have had the whooping cough vaccine. I was very shocked and very hurt and upset. I sat next to his bed and clasped my hands in prayer asking for strength to get through this. They sent us home with medication and said if there is any change and it's not working, call right away.

When we arrived home, mum and I took it in turns to look after George. Jacob was away at work when this all started up. He was nearing the end of his time away and would soon be home. Every day, we were helping George as he was fitting regularly, at least 30 fits a day and I was frantic. After we had been home a month, I called the doctor, who was based at Raigmore Hospital, and he arranged for a helicopter to take us to Aberdeen Hospital. I was told to pack a bag and the helicopter would meet us at the airfield near Dornoch in about two hours. Mum agreed to look after Tanya, while I was away with George.

The two hours went very quickly, and I was waiting with George at the airfield. I looked up as I heard a loud noise approaching. Here was a medical helicopter, yellow and with flashing lights. As it landed, I was told to duck my head down as we approached the helicopter. George was strapped to a stretcher and rigged up with oxygen and his own little headphones. I was told to sit next to my little boy, I had tears in my eyes, worried what was going to happen. The pilot and the paramedics in the plane tried to reassure me and we were away up in the air…

We landed in about fifteen minutes, and I was amazed it was so fast. The pilot passed me a wee teddy bear pilot for George.

"Good luck to you both." After exited the helicopter, he was rushed inside on a stretcher to a trolley bed. I placed the teddy on the bed with George. They did more tests and came up with the same answer as Raigmore. The whooping cough vaccination had triggered the meningitis off. They said that he was partly brain damaged through this and he also had cerebral palsy. I was totally shocked and in floods of tears at this. The doctor then continued, he will need special schooling and he will also need toilet pads for the rest of his life. We will be giving you a wheelchair too as he will never walk in his life! She asked me if I was on my own, as I will need a lot of support and help through this situation. I replied that I had my dear mother who was an ex-nurse was helping me with my daughter too. My husband was working away and is back soon. She said that I would need their help, as he would need speech therapy and physiotherapy to work on his legs and arms to get him stronger. She wished me all the best and that she would be sending her report to the paediatricians at Raigmore Hospital, who was dealing with George's case. We had the wheelchair ready for him as well. Again, she said that she was sorry she didn't have any good news for me. Such a lovely little boy for this to happen to him.

We returned home by land ambulance with George strapped into his new wheelchair. I thanked the driver as he left and as mum came out, I cried so much on her shoulder, that she held me tightly. Mum asked me what the diagnosis was.

I sniffled and said, "They say he has cerebral palsy and partial brain damage. He isn't allowed anymore jags. He is to have a lot of nursing care day and night, physiotherapy, and speech therapy. How will I cope, Mum?"

Mum just smiled, as she did, sweetly and said, "God will find a way, you'll see. Put your faith and trust in Him."

Jacob came home and was equally shocked to find out what had happened. He was unable to cope with it, so he went to the pub.

I gave up my job to look after George, as I couldn't concentrate at work and was always turning up looking like a zombie. They said that I should put my family first. George was my priority and Tanya was being cared for by mum.

So, every day, I was attending George morning and night. I would be lucky if I got any decent sleep at all. I was nursing him through his fits and sickness and regular nappy changing. I got a call from the physiotherapist, who was also going to be visiting weekly. We were working together trying to get strength back into his legs to enable him to walk.

It was exceedingly difficult as he was screaming and fitting through it all. We persevered.

Jacob, my husband, struggled with the situation and wanting me to put George into a care home. One day, I walked into George's bedroom while he was in his cot and his father was standing over him, holding a pillow very tightly hovering over George staring at him intently. I shouted at him.

"What do you think you're doing?"

Jacob looked at me scared and said, "Isn't this better for him?"

"You will not kill him. Trying to smother your son is murder!" I cried. He dropped the pillow on the floor and ran from the room. I shouted after him and told him to get out and never come back.

I packed his bags, while he was away at sea and went to see a solicitor to file for a divorce. The solicitor was shocked at the reasons for the divorce. But we went ahead with it. As Jacob arrived back from his work, he looked at me glumly and said, "It's him or me!" I chose George.

He collected his bags and trudged away. The divorce was quickly granted. Now, I was free again and I was left with Tanya and my little boy George to care for.

Chapter 9
Three Is a Magic Number?

Days turned into months and Mary the physiotherapist and I were working extremely hard to get George's muscles in his legs and feet working. We also spent time with his arms and grip. Mum also helped us both and looking after Tanya, while we worked with George. The doctors and consultants were all incredibly surprised that George was walking, taking steps, and moving his legs for himself. They were very complimentary of our decent work with him, especially the doctor who gave us the wheelchair.

We proved them all wrong. George still had to take lots of packets of powder to calm his fits, but it was stable of sorts. The other thing which he found exceptionally hard was his speech therapy, but we persevered. As he grew older and more mobile, he was accepted in a special school. He was coming on in leaps and bounds. The teachers were all extremely impressed with him, and they all said they loved working with him, such a pleasant little boy, despite his difficulties.

One day, I was shocked to the core from the contents of a letter dropped onto the carpet. Someone had nominated me for 'carer of the year.' I received a certificate and a letter commending me for all the excellent work I had done for George, as well as holding down a good home for Tanya.

I went to see my mum with the children and showed her the letter and certificate and she smiled and said, "Well done. You have earned it. You have the patience of a saint dealing with all this. All those months with truly little sleep, with George growing stronger and cheekier."

The teachers at the special school decided to give George a special trike to keep using his legs and exercising regularly. I was pleased with this, but the local children all took the mick out of George, and I went out and shouted at them.

"He has cerebral palsy!" I spoke. But to them, this meant nothing. This put George off bringing the bike home again. I was so heartbroken and upset at this nasty treatment by the other kids. I persuaded George to try the bike again and this time, he got used to the kids laughing at him and he was proud that he had a bike and even getting home before the other kids. The ridicule stopped eventually and as he grew older; he grew out of the bike, and we had to hand it back for another young disabled boy to use.

As time went on, I was telling my mum how happy I was that the kids were growing up and everything was running smoothly, but I was incredibly lonely. I love my kids so much, but I felt I needed another adult to be a companion.

She said, "I know, Heather Ann, you will find happiness one day, the world is a big place and I'm sure there's someone out there for you. When you find happiness again, I won't stand in your way and if you need me, I will always be here for you and my grandchildren." I thanked her and we hugged.

As it so happened the next week, I bought a newspaper, *The Press and Journal*. In the personal ads were lots of men and women looking for pen pals and happiness and maybe more. These drew me in and for the very first time ever, I decided to answer one of them. He was staying in Inverness; he was a head chef in Aviemore High Range Hotel. So, I wrote a short letter to him introducing myself. After a short while, I received a letter back. It was a genuinely nice handwritten letter, expressing his need to look for a long-term partner to share his life with, as he too was very lonely. He had included his phone number too. We started chatting on the phone and things were progressing quite well and he suggested that we meet up for a meal. So, I agreed and asked mum if she wouldn't mind looking after the children for a few hours. I told her that I was going to Inverness for a meal with my new pen pal.

She said, "That's fine but be very careful."

I was nervous of meeting this man, as I had never seen him before, and we had only spoken on the phone. I got dressed up and put on my makeup and headed for the bus. As I arrived in Inverness, I was very shaky and nervous and went to the train station to meet my pen pal. This man walked up to me, and asked if I was Heather Ann?

I said, "I am."

He introduced himself as Daniel. I was incredibly nervous, and he was quite clearly shy. I said that I must be back for 7 as mum was looking after my children. He said he was fine with that.

It was a glorious sunny day in Inverness, quite a few people were milling about. I felt like I was Cinderella going to the ball and having to be home sharp at 7 p.m. or I wouldn't be allowed out again. So, we went for our meal, and we shared our stories with each other. We had a really enjoyable time together and we had a lovely walk around Inverness. We stopped off at a pub near the train station for a few drinks before I had to catch my bus. When he had bought me a drink, he left me saying he would be back in a minute. I felt like a right lemon, being stood up. Until he walked back in with a massive bunch of flowers and a bottle of whisky for mum for letting me out to meet him and for looking after the kids. In the bag with the whisky, was a little card, saying thank you to my mum, that he was delighted at meeting me, her daughter and that he hoped to meet her in the future too. I had to go then, and he walked me to the bus stop, and he shook my hand and said he hoped to see me again soon.

All the way home, I was thinking of him and the lovely gifts he had bought both for me and my mum. I thought this was it, happiness again, after being so long without a man in my life. As I arrived home, I gave mum her gift of the whisky and showed off my flowers in a vase. I also handed her the card, and she was pleased. "How lovely, flowers and whisky, sounds like a real gentleman. He also wants to see you again too. Wow! We'll have to invite him up to meet your children and to meet me. We can all have dinner together and get to know him." I phoned him and asked him if he would like to come and meet the family. I gave him mum's phone number as he asked for it and he called her. He was very pleasant on the phone and asked if it was possible to come up and see mum and me and the kids? Mum said, "Yes, of course, come and meet the family."

The day soon arrived, and he knocked at the door. I answered it with a shy smile. He shook my hand again and said with a smile, "Hello again." He made a bee line for George and Tanya and gave each of them a small gift. They were rather shy at meeting him. Mum smiled as he introduced himself and she thanked him personally for his gifts. Mum called us through for the meal and the kids were smiling and they said thank you for their toys. He told us all about his job and where he stays in Inverness. Everything went well. After dinner, he said thank you to mum and said that he would love to come again. Mum said that he was most welcome in her house. She also told him to be patient with me as I have had two bad marriages before. He said, "Of course, I will take it very slowly. There's no rush." Then he was away.

In the kitchen after he had gone, we were tidying up by washing and drying the dishes.

I said to mum, "Honestly, Mum, what did you think of him?"

She said, "He seems genuinely nice. I hope that this is the one for you!"

"Yes, me too, Mum." I packed up the kids' stuff and took them home just a few doors up. They were chatting about Daniel and how nice he was buying them new toys. As we went inside, Tanya asked, "When we would see him again?" I said hopefully soon. She said, "When you think he is ok and good with us, you can ask him to stay. Night, Mum."

I was pleasantly surprised at what she said.

Days and nights were passing fast working with George and his mobility. I got to thinking, one night after I had put George to bed, whether I should invite Daniel up to stay for the weekend to get to know us, as a family, a wee bit more. The next morning, I mentioned it to Tanya, and she was incredibly pleased and excited about it. I also mentioned it to Mum, and she said that would be nice, then he will get to know you all better. As luck would have it, he called mum's number asking if I was about, I took the phone and asked him if he was available to come up and stay for the weekend? He was delighted and said he would see us on Friday night. "It's a date," I replied, blushing.

On the Friday, he turned up and knocked on the door. Tanya was first to the door, and he smiled and came in. We enjoyed a nice supper together.

Tanya turned to Daniel and said, "Are you going with my mum?"

He smiled and said, "Would you like me to?"

"Yes! But, if you do, you will have to treat her well and love her well, as she had a troubled marriage with my dad."

He said, "Of course, I will, I will be nice to your mum and you two as well." The weekend finished all too quickly and as he was about to leave, he gave the kids a hug each and asked me if I wanted to stay with him the next weekend. I said I would like that if mum can mind the children. He said, "We could see how we get on more, but if you don't want to stay, I understand."

He smiled and offered his hand, but I gave him a hug instead. After he was gone, I was tidying up when Tanya said, "If this love is pure, are you going to let him into your heart?"

I shrugged and smiled. That got me thinking awfully hard. What if he is true to what he says he is? Could we really have a good relationship, better than the previous two?

I was working with George for the whole week with Mary the physiotherapist who George had taken a dislike to, because of the hurt from the treatment being conducted. He didn't understand she was helping him. We were both exhausted by the end of the week. So much so, that I was glad mum said she would mind the kids for the night when I went to stay with Daniel down in Inverness. He understood that the kids came first and with the challenges dealing with George's needs.

We had a great day and night and I said to him that he was welcome every weekend if he wanted?

He was delighted with this and pecked me on the cheek for the first time.

The next weekend he came up, the first of many weekend visits. The kids were getting used to seeing him every week. So, one night when he was up with us, we had a chat about him coming up to live with us for good. He was good with the kids, and I was starting to fall for him. The kids were smiling when I asked him. We discovered he had a mortgage with an old woman friend of his and he said he was going to sell her his share. I told mum not to worry as this is going to be well as we both understood each other.

Several months had passed since my first correspondence with Daniel and here was the day he was moving in with us. Everything was going fine. He bought a pet hamster for Tanya, at which she was delighted. He also took George out for walks in his wheelchair. One thing led to another and soon, I found out I was pregnant. I was scared to tell him after the unpleasant experience I had with Jacob my ex-husband. But I had no need to worry, as when I told him he was over the moon and incredibly happy and excited. We invited Mum over and told the whole family our good news.

Daniel was beaming and said to mum, "I would like to marry your lovely daughter, Katie, and make this marriage work, so the child she is carrying will have a mum and a dad."

Mum said, "Don't ever treat her bad or the kids as she went through enough before!"

He replied positively, "I will make this marriage work well and I don't intend to let anyone down."

Mum smiled and the kids laughed, and everyone was happy about it.

As time went on, and I was four months gone, Jonas had asked me to take him into Inverness to get his bus to Aberdeen for the ship to get to the rigs. I was ok with that. Mum and I were going to go shopping in Inverness for our outfits, Daniel was ok with minding the kids. We got a big hug and kiss from each of them, and I collected mum from only a few doors up and Daniel called Jonas to say we were on the way.

So, we set off. We were very excited to be going to Inverness shopping for our wedding outfits, we turned onto the A9 southbound, and we were about to turn right headed to Lednabirichen, my indicators were flashing as I slowed to make the turn, when the car lurched forward with an almighty crash as a Mercedes car smashed right into the back of me.

I was visibly shocked and very worried and sore especially as there were no airbags in the vehicle.

I turned to mum and said, "Are you ok?"

She said, "My chest is sore. What the hell happened?"

She got out of the car and swore. She noticed the damage to the car went over to the driver of the other car terribly angry saying, "Why did you do that to her car? She is four months pregnant!"

He apologised and said, "I was rushing to Raigmore Hospital for a check over." He began to shake.

His wife chimed in, "Yes and I was telling him to slow down, but no! He knows best and now look!"

I opened the door very gingerly and tried to stand but I felt contractions beginning. No! It's too early! Someone had called the police and an ambulance. I heard the sirens but was focusing on what was happening. The car was a total mess and a write-off.

The ambulance and police finally arrived after what seemed like an age. I had a genuinely nice police officer sat in my car with me as I needed to sit down as the contractions were getting stronger. He said, "Hold on, love, help is here."

I thought that I was going to lose this baby and I was heartbroken.

I prayed and I prayed for the baby to be ok. I was rushed onto a stretcher, and they did the first checks and Mum, and I went in one ambulance and the other driver's wife went into another. We were taken to the Lawson Hospital in Golspie, which was the nearest. I was taken to a bed and had drips put in to try and stop the contractions as this was way too early for a birth. The doctor wasn't very happy and said, "It will be a miracle if this works, I'm not sure if we can stop baby wanting out just now."

To be honest, I had little time for God, but this accident had led to me praying hard like never before. Tears were dripping down my face and I just felt helpless. I was there for nine hours with the drips being constantly changed. Mum and the wife of the other driver both had suffered whiplash and were being treated not too far away. The doctor had called Daniel, Leslie and Jonas to inform them that we had been involved in a crash. They had all panicked as they saw the police and the wrecked car being towed away. The doctor had told us the baby's survival chances were 50/50.

The police officer who was talking to me at the scene came in and wanted a wee chat with me. I told him everything that happened, and the officer said, "If you had children in the back, they would all be dead as the seatbelts were ripped out by the force of the impact and your mum's handbag was embedded in the windscreen. It looked like it had been in the back but was thrown forward with the impact. He must have been going well over 75-80MPH. You were both so lucky to be alive especially with you being pregnant." I cried and cried. "Someone must have been looking after you there."

"Yes, you're right there. It could have been so much worse. The car is a write-off, but at least we're still here. I am so grateful to you all. A car is only a piece of metal, nothing else matters apart from my family," I spoke.

The officer then stood up and said, "The driver will be charged with speeding and being over the drink-drive limit. Now, don't you be worrying about anything and please rest up and look after that precious bundle you are carrying." I said thank you and he nodded and turned to leave the room.

I was allowed to leave the hospital that night as the baby was now stable. Leslie and Jonas came to pick us up, to take us home. Mum still had whiplash, but it had now subsided.

We were all chatting in the car about the accident, and we were all so glad that Tanya and George weren't in the car. That would have been more of a disaster! I was told by the police the seatbelts were ripped completely out of the back and the thing that saved us was the tow bar.

Mum also said the same as the policeman, "Someone up there must be looking after you."

I said, "I know, Mum, it's a miracle."

The wedding grew much closer and the memory of the car crash was dimming, thankfully. We had been to Inverness on the bus and got our outfits. We were getting married at the registry office, as Daniel wanted it that way. Everything went very well, until later my wedding night. An ambulance had to be called, as I was spotting with blood. They rushed me into the Raigmore Hospital, and I was admitted to the maternity unit. They gave me an injection to calm me down. Then a scan was taken of the baby.

The nurse said, "She is doing ok."

"Oh, so it is she then?"

"Yes, sorry, I thought you knew."

"No!"

"You do now!" she sniggered, as she turned and walked away. I breathed a huge sigh of relief and rubbed my distended belly and said I will be glad when you are out and in my arms. I slept quite well through the night and awoke to see the consultants and nurses at the foot of the bed. I was startled and asked what the matter was. The nurse said, "We're very sorry but you're going to have to stay with us for the full term of your pregnancy, as you need total bed rest."

I groaned, "Oh no!"

He said, "Oh, yes. Or your baby might not make it."

I phoned Daniel and mum with the news, and they arranged everything.

Now, in hospital, it seems timeless, and the weeks flew by and now came the day for her to arrive. I must have been pushing for quite a few hours. The midwives were coming in regularly and they were concerned that I wasn't dilating fast enough. After referring to a senior medical person, they called a surgeon in, and they decided that I would need a C section to move things on a bit as the baby was in distress. I asked them to contact my husband Daniel to come to the hospital. He drove our car to the hospital. Having been gowned up, he joined me in the operating theatre while they were trying to get the baby out. Eventually, they got her out. She was an extremely healthy beautiful baby. I was so thankful to the staff, and I thanked God that she was born safely, especially after everything that had happened and in particular, the car crash. I had to stay in hospital for a week for recovery and to let the stitches heal.

After that week passed, I was allowed home.

Once home and settled, there was a knock at the door, and it was the police officer who was dealing with the car crash. He came in and asked me if I was ok? We offered him tea, but he just said that he came to see how I was doing after he had heard I had given birth to the baby especially after that stupid man who had been drinking and speeding had nearly taken her from me.

I said, "Here she is!"

He was smiling and pleased that she was finally born safely. "It's thanks to you for helping me to calm down," I said.

He modestly replied that he was just him doing his duty.

We decided to call the baby Caitlyn.

Chapter 10
Temper, Tempest

Time moved on and it was soon time for Caitlyn to have her injections and I was incredibly nervous. She had no side effects, so we were relieved. As she was growing older, we needed a bigger home. We were given a four-bedroomed house in Invergordon.

So, in this new house, the children each had their own rooms. Tanya was in High School, while George was still in his special school at St Duthus, and he was so much stronger now. Caitlyn was with me until she started playschool and then nursery.

I was busy working and Daniel was looking after the kids. As the weekend came closer, we decided we would visit Dornoch to see my friend Marge and my mum. While we were there, mum got a call saying that Jacques and his friend Alex were coming up as well. I thought that that would be lovely to see them both again.

There was a roar of engines when they both arrived. Mum invited them in, and she prepared a meal, as they had had a long journey.

Jacques was wondering about my friend Marge. We all went out to the pub including my husband, Daniel. My friend was there, and we all had a great time reminiscing about the past.

After a few hours, Daniel got up and said, "Up the road now! Get Home!"

I had never seen him like this. I said, "No! I'm staying with my friends."

He snarled, "If you don't get up that road now, I will not be happy!"

I said, "Look,, Daniel, I will go up after I have finished my drinks on the table."

Then he shouted and was so nasty. I was so ashamed. Jacques stood up and said to him, "Look pal, can you take your good lady's word." He looked at him and said nothing. He was so red faced; I had never seen him like that before. Then he stormed off.

When we had finished our drinks, we left to walk up to Mum's. She was minding the kids. I heard a lot of shouting when we were close to the house. Mum was outside looking red faced. I asked her, "What on Earth is going on?"

She said, "Talk to your husband. He tried to take Caitlyn out of her bed in the early hours to go to the swing park. The man is crazy! I tried to stop him, but he went off his head and booted me in the legs."

When Jacques heard mum say this, he said, "Wait until I get the little s***e."

He and his mate went hunting for him.

Luckily, Caitlyn was still asleep and never heard this. The time now was 3 a.m. and he could have done anything to harm my family. This was a different side to the man I loved. I did not like it.

The next morning, Jacques came to see me before he left.

"If you have any bother again with him and he lays one finger on you, let me know and we'll be up to see to him"

I said, "It's the drink that did it." Jacques said, "Aye! He showed his true colours, is what he did."

We hugged and said our goodbyes and Jacques was off.

I said, "We had better be off too, Mum, sorry again."

But she said, "You have no need to be sorry for anything. You take care of these wee ones, and I will hopefully see you soon."

Time passed without further incident and Daniel seemed genuinely sorry for his actions and was determined to make amends. The festive season came, and we had a wonderful Christmas with our neighbours. We were also invited into the neighbour's house for New Year celebrations. Life was going wonderfully again.

Caitlyn was growing up and started her schooling at nursery. But during her time at nursery, they decided that she needed special schooling as she was not as advanced as it should be for her age. She was diagnosed with a learning difficulty.

She then attended St Duthus' special school in Tain a few days a week. She required one to one teaching. I was very disheartened at the thought of this service and how it looked to people and asked my husband Daniel, "Why?"

He just said, "It's what is provided for those that need it. She is only at St Duthus' for a couple of days at a time as the normal primary school is too fast for her brain to take in."

Caitlyn started having severe bowel problems at the age of six years. The specialist said that it was a lazy bowel, and they made her take bottles of medication every night, to clear her bowel out.

I was working permanent night shifts at the time and Caitlyn was begging to stay and not leave her with her father. I didn't understand why, as she never said anything to me specific. She kept writing me lovely poems and was always so clingy to me and always telling me that she loved me. Her bowel problems were still ongoing and became erratic, gone one minute and back with a vengeance the next. She was always saying that her belly was sore and didn't want to go to school but would eventually go. Her bowels were getting worse, and I was also being told to use suppositories as her bottom was very red and sore. The specialists were all puzzled and were wondering why it was a lazy bowel. The work at school gradually got too much for Caitlyn, so the primary school said enough is enough and sent her to St Duthus' full time.

As a married woman, I became puzzled at my husband who decided to sleep in the spare room instead of sleeping with me. I was distraught and was left wondering what the reason was for this change.

One day, I was returning from work, and we were having a few drinks at home. Tanya was out at a disco. Daniel had given her money to go. Caitlyn and George were upstairs in their rooms. Daniel got a phone call from his sister. I was in the kitchen making a drink when he came in behind me attacking me and fighting with me. I tried to push him off, but he grabbed my neck and slammed my head into the kitchen units repeatedly until my face was bleeding and bruised. I was trying to fight back, but his strength overpowered me. During the shouting and fighting, Caitlyn phoned my mum and told her what was happening. He then grabbed a kitchen knife and plunged it into my shoulder and my arm. I was on the floor bleeding, and he was still yelling.

Mum had told Caitlyn to go to her room and hide, she called the police. I managed to run outside, and he locked the door behind me, swearing. I yelled at him to let the kids go, but he refused. I tried to get round the back, but he had locked all the doors. I could see the children at the windows screaming. George had both ears covered by his hands. The police arrived and while they attended me, until an ambulance arrived, other police cars arrived and the police ordered Daniel to open the door, or they would break it down. I could hear yelling inside as the kids were pleading with him to let them go.

A short while later, there was still a standoff!

The police told him to let the kids go and to turn himself in. They approached the front door of the house with a red battering ram they called the Key.

But the door opened and in they went. There was a lot of shouting and fighting. As the ambulance crew were tending me, he was being carried out, kicking, and screaming all four limbs were bound and he was swearing like a trooper. They threw him in the police van, and they locked him in and slammed the door. He was kicking and screaming inside the van as it drove away. There were six officers who had carried him out and they were looking tired and bruised. They told me he was going to jail and court in the morning. He was also resisting arrest.

The ambulance crew were satisfied that I was well enough to be allowed to stay home, as I didn't want to be taken to hospital as there was nobody to look after the kids. They had stitched up the knife wounds and stopped the bleeding. I was left to go into my house. The police officer came to me and apologised for the mess and the CID would be here in the morning to take photos. With that he bid me a goodnight and they were off.

I walked into the house and there was signs of a struggle and things were all over the place. We tidied up and I hugged and kissed the kids and reassured them that he wouldn't be coming back again. I told them that the police have taken him away and he will be in court tomorrow.

I began to make a cup of tea when Tanya walked in all happy after the disco. She was shocked when she saw my two black eyes and I told her what had happened. I explained everything and she was angry that she wasn't here to help me. We all had a hug and a weep and after a ciggy, I went to bed.

The next day, I heard a knock at the door, and it was two men in identical clothing. They were CID and they took photos of my face and shoulder wounds. They said they were surprised; I was still alive. It could have been much worse. I asked whether he would be coming back here? They said that he would never be allowed back here or anywhere near here. They thanked me for my honesty and left. As they were leaving, mum arrived—just after I had put my sunglasses on. She hugged me softly as I yelped when she got near the stitches. She was totally shocked and when I removed my sunglasses, she was in tears.

"My poor girl, what has he done to you? I hope you won't ever have him back."

"Of course not!" I said.

He appeared in court charged with actual bodily harm and he was asked to declare in court, and he said guilty. Because he said that, they just fined him £1000 and ordered him never to return to Invergordon or anywhere near me. He left to go to his brothers in Glasgow. I was shocked when the police officer came round and told me the sentence. He thought it was bad and the sentencing a joke, but they would be keeping an eye on me and my family from now on.

Once more, our lives became quite normal, and the kids were getting on well with their schooling and things were starting to settle down. Although we didn't have a man in the house, everything ran smoothly, and my home and work life were easier than before. It was great that mum helped by, looking after Caitlyn and George while I was away. I decided to sandblast the walls in the house on my own and was amazed at the finished product. I got new flooring and a new fitted kitchen. Everything was going great.

Caitlyn was starting to enjoy her school in Tain and the teachers were overly impressed with progress. She was a proper teacher's pet. When her work was done, she would help some of the children with Down's Syndrome. Tanya was doing well in school; George was also improving at school as well. Life couldn't have been better, but as time marched on, I was happy with the children coming on, but I was again feeling lonely. Every night, the kids would sit with me and keep me company for a wee while and when they went up, I was just longing for an adult conversation. This continued for a period of five years. Although every few months, the police officer who looked after me visited us to see how we were getting on. He even tried to ask me out, but, I refused, he was not my type!

I was working nights and days now and I was happy in my work. I came home one day, and Caitlyn told me that she had seen how lonely I was. She had also been receiving texts and messages on Facebook from her father Daniel. I was surprised and annoyed at this as she hadn't told me. He had been telling her that he was a changed man and had counselling and he was a much better man for it, and he was sorry for what had happened. I was unsure about this, and I was stuck. Daniel messaged me and we began to talk again. He said I thought that you would have had a divorce by now. But I said, I believe in marriage and wouldn't change the name. I had asked about a divorce, but the solicitor had said it would cost £1000. I could never have afforded that. He said that he was quite pleased with that.

We decided to go on a date in Inverness. I was very wary and unsure, but he tried to put me at my ease. He bought me flowers and said I looked lovely. He was saying all the right things and he was very charming again. Over the next few weeks, we had several meals out and we decided to say to the kids we would be getting back together. Caitlyn was overjoyed and George and Tanya were wary of him, but he later talked them round. He promised that he was doing things differently. I told Mum last, and she was furious. Eventually, she agreed that it was my life and I had to make my own choices and maybe mistakes. He moved back in, and everything was going well. He even slept with me for a few months. But then, he needed his own space, and I was a very disturbed sleeper. I was disappointed, but at least, he was here with us and sharing the bills.

Caitlyn was working in Candles Made in Tain. She was helping to make the candles and was so pleased with herself. She even brought one home for us. Her best friend was working the till in the front of the shop. I often visited her at work in the shop and she was incredibly happy in her work. Daniel was hardly chatty anymore.

Caitlyn joined Invergordon Academy at twelve years of age. Everything was going well although she was still needing extra help there. She was happy, as her friends from the other primary school were also there. Suddenly, her bowels clogged up. She was very poorly and had daily visits to the doctors. They sent her to the bowel specialist in Raigmore who asked her why this had happened again. Caitlyn shrugged her shoulders and stared at the floor. I don't know. They even asked me, and I said I wish I knew. The specialists were asking if anyone was stressing her at school.

She looked at her dad with fear in her eyes and answered "No!"

The specialist asked, "Is anything stressful at home?" Again, she stared at the floor, and I thought it was me causing the bowel problems while I was at work. I said that to her. She looked at me then the specialist and she said I just like to have my mam there at home with us. Daniel shook his head.

"She was given strong medicine to keep the bowels going." He explained, "If the bladder is working well, the bowels have won't have problems and vice versa." She had so many accidents at school she was always taking a spare change of clothing. To make it worse, she was diagnosed with an age differential. She had a label now with a mental age of eight.

There was a teacher's meeting at which they said if she didn't have these health problems, she would be coming on lovely. Next time she must go to hospital, we'll send you homework for her to do in hospital, so she won't fall behind anymore. One day, Caitlyn said, "I am not going to school anymore."

I asked her, "Why?" but she tried to hide it. I asked her again and she said the kids are picking on her calling her names. This was really upsetting for her, and she was almost a teenager. I just wished that they would understand it was not her fault. Kids can be so cruel. Caitlyn was given special pads to wear from the hospital. She also had a health assistant, who came to see how she was doing. She started to get on better with the pads. She also felt better as she was having pads the same as her brother George.

As we were settled now in our Invergordon home, we were starting to make friends. The lady who worked for Provident, who came round weekly, asked us to come to her party. Her family and friends will be there, and it would be good to get to know more people. We both agreed. I asked mum if she would mind the kids that weekend and she said that she would.

On the Friday night, we were dressed and getting dinner ready for the kids. Tanya was away for the weekend with her friends. With only Caitlyn and George, mum would find it easier. She said to Daniel, "Watch her in case she drinks too much."

He said, "Not to worry, she is in fine hands with me." We got into the taxi and were off. The night was good, great music, great disco. Everyone was very friendly and having fun. I was fine inside the house, but, as I began to leave, I felt strange and very dizzy. I must have fallen over a few times, I banged my head. Daniel was shouting at me and dragging me through grass and parkland. I was yelling at him to leave me alone. I felt awful still and guessed that my drink had been spiked, however, he was fine. I remember everything, he grabbed me and started pushing me against a fence. He was groping me and pushing hard at me. I was on my period and told him to leave me alone. But he kept on, tearing at my underwear, and trying to have sex with me. I kept fighting back and saying, "No," but no reply. It must have been a miracle as he couldn't get going and the taxi pulled round the corner. He swore at me, as if it was my fault. I was relieved but bruised and battered. It could have been so much worse, and I could have been raped instead of just attempted rape.

The ride home in the taxi was quiet and I couldn't look at him. He was sighing and grumpy. When we arrived at home, I could barely walk and the taxi driver said, "Are you ok?"

Daniel said, "Yes, she is fine." I must have looked a sight with my tights ripped along with my blouse and skirt. I felt dirty and ashamed.

Daniel said, "Go inside, I will pay him."

I staggered up to bed and we never spoke all night. I couldn't sleep very well, and my arm was becoming swollen. In the morning, it was so bad, I could barely move it. I went to the hospital with Daniel, and he warned me not to say anything. I was called through and he was left in the waiting room. The nurse cleaned me up and pulled the broken glass from my face and cleaned up my grazed legs. As she had done that, I had an x-ray which showed I had broken my wrist in two places. They asked me, "How did this happen?" I told a lie; I fell of my bike and went off balance and went over the handlebars. I'm sure they didn't believe me, as the nurse said, "You have a slight concussion. Are you sure, you don't want to change your story? I can see you're frightened"

I went to get my arm plastered and said it again, "I want it left at that." They were whispering in a corner, and they were looking at me all the time. I think they must have known but can't do anything without my say. How foolish. I would have the cast on my arm for four weeks, so I had to have time off on sick leave.

The four weeks dragged, and I was so happy to get back to work after the four weeks. I was only back at work for a few nights when Caitlyn started to act strangely. She was very clingy, and I asked her if everything was ok? She looked down at the ground and said, "Yes!"

I said, "Is it me?"

She said, "Yes, I don't like you going on night shift, as I miss you."

Daniel came in and said, "You don't need to miss your mam, as she will not get time to miss you, as she will be very busy at work." As the days went by, I was blissfully unaware of anything wrong.

One day, I was on a day off work and Caitlyn was not well and feeling sick. I took her to the doctors, and they said it could be a sick bug. She was then off school for some time. When she finally recovered and she went back to school, everything started off well. But little did I know that things were starting to get worse. The teacher noticed that she was struggling at school, and I was called into the school. As I was shown into the head's office, the teachers and the head were chatting. The teacher said, "Is there a problem at home or school?" Caitlyn was never good at telling anyone what was wrong with her, apart from the fact that she wasn't coping with me not being with her. This was an ongoing problem, but we could find no solution. Why was Caitlyn hiding things from me? As she got older things got worse.

Once more, I was going on a night shift and I was handed a little note, which said, "Mam, I will always love you and I miss you loads." I was very puzzled and quite worried, especially after I showed the note to the staff at break time. They told me that they thought Caitlyn was trying to tell you something is wrong, but she doesn't know how to. I thanked them and said I will find out. I even found myself praying through the shift that nothing bad was going on while I am at work.

When I returned home, I asked Daniel if he had had a good night with no problems. He said, "Yes of course, I had to take the mobile from Caitlyn while you are on night shift just in case, she texts you too much."

I went upstairs to see her and sat on her bed. I asked her if everything is ok. She gingerly said, "Yes, but dad took away my mobile!" I looked at the bed sheets and there was a fresh stain which looked like blackcurrant, with a dark and bright red colour on the edges. There was also a wee bit of sick also. I asked her once more, "Why are you so ill? When I go away to work, you still say nothing."

I decided to take her to the doctors again and he examined her carefully. He said she may need a suppository up her back passage to release some pressure of her bowel to move. We returned home and I tried to put the suppository in place, but she wouldn't relax for me. I also noticed that it was all red and I asked her what happened. She looked down at the floor and said she didn't know. The teachers were coming regularly with books and homework for her to do while she wasn't at school. She still insisted on not going to school as she wasn't coping with this. After things had seemed to have settled down, I thought it had.

The time came for Caitlyn to return to the school, and she was comfortable about returning. The head teacher said that it would be better in class than always at home. I agreed. So, Caitlyn returned to school, everything was going well and as I was on night shift, it meant that I could walk her to school. She only allowed me to go halfway though.

I spoke to Daniel, "Why is she so sick all the time? It can't be just about me leaving her to go to work at night."

He said in a sarcastic tone, "You know when a dog is sick all the time, you take it to the vets and have it put down."

I was shocked when he said that about his only daughter. It still makes me shudder.

When Caitlyn came home, I told her what her dad had said.

She just shook her head and said, "More like he needs to be put down!"

I was again shocked, but just said, "Why did you say that?"

She just shrugged her shoulders and said, "Never mind, Mam, it's ok."

I said to Daniel, "You should let her have friends over to spend time with her while I am working."

He said, "No! She doesn't need friends."

I knew not to argue.

Yet again, I spoke to Daniel, "Why do you not come into the marital bedroom?"

He said, "No, I'm quite happy in the box room, so I can sleep better. I can't seem to sleep with you."

I said. "Well, isn't it funny? When we're on holiday, you sleep with me."

He just laughed and said, "I'm more relaxed on holiday."

So once more, on my days off, I was on my own in my bedroom thinking—what kind of married life is this? I prayed for it to change, but nothing ever happened. I said to God, "I feel like a prostitute and a slave to my own husband." That went on for an awfully long time. I just had to make do with my Bible to read.

Caitlyn came home from school with her friend and said, "As it's the weekend, can I have my friend staying with me?"

I said, "Yes, you can, but don't make much noise."

Her friend said, "Does your mum not sleep with your dad?"

Caitlyn said, "No! He doesn't want to sleep with her because she is restless in bed."

Her friend said, "That's weird, because when you are married, you should always sleep together."

One day, we were upstairs, and I was in Caitlyn's room and Caitlyn was not well again. Daniel was standing on the landing and Caitlyn said to me, "You should push him down the stairs!"

I shook my head and said, "No! Why?" Caitlyn just shrugged her shoulders. He went down the stairs to make dinner and I quietly asked her why she wanted me to do that as it would kill him!

She said, "Good! Because I don't like him, I hate him." I asked why but she just clammed up.

Her bowels were continuing to block up. I had to take her to see the bowel specialist and they were continuing with her; she must be stressed at home. I kept saying there is no stress

166

at home. She just doesn't want to be left alone with her dad while I'm on nights. I was asked if I could change my shifts to days. Maybe, this might be the answer to it all. Things started to settle down within days of me changing to days.

One night, Caitlyn was in her bed, and I was just getting ready for bed. Caitlyn called me in and said that her belly was sore again and she just couldn't cope with it again. The next day, I made an appointment with the doctor, and he examined her belly. I was asked if I wouldn't mind leaving the room for him to have a chat with Caitlyn in private. I was puzzled but, I agreed.

I said, "You might get more answers than we do."

I was sent to the waiting room and was there for quite some time. He called me in and asked Caitlyn to wait outside the room. I asked him, "What is wrong with her?" He said that he asked Caitlyn if she was having sex behind your back as she is fully sexually active. My face fell and I was filled with fear. I hope not! She is very much underage. He said that he just needed to ask that. He gave her meds for her bowels again as she was totally constipated. She was also discharging, and he said she will come into full periods soon. So, I asked her when we came out of the doctors.

She said, "Change it, Mam. I am not doing anything wrong. My dad loves me and cares for me when you go to work."

I said to her, "If someone is doing terrible things to her, would she tell me?" She said, "Yes," she would. Then she completely changed the subject. I was really worried now and planned to talk to Daniel when we got home. But Caitlyn specifically asked me not to tell him anything what the doctors said.

I asked, "Why?"

She just said, "He won't be very happy."

I just said, "Why? You should look up to your dad. Are you scared of him?"

Caitlyn spoke in a scared voice, "Yes!"

When we got home, I told Daniel what the doctors had said, and his face went red with temper.

"How dare he say that about Caitlyn? Just wait till I see him, I'll teach him". He raged.

I said, "Just leave it, he must have got it wrong." He sat quietly raging about it for a long time. I was wondering why he was so angry about it. What on Earth could it be to make him lose his temper at just that?

As I went to my bed that night, Caitlyn was in bed watching TV and George was in with her. Tanya was away staying at a friend's house. I said goodnight to everyone and to the dog Troy in his cage in the kitchen. He got all excited thinking I would ask him upstairs, but he looked sad when I told him bed. As I was getting settled into bed, I heard Troy barking and growling, then Daniel was shouting and then a wee yelp. I shouted, "What's wrong with the dog?" Daniel just said he's playing with the dog. After a few hours, I heard Troy going mental in his cage. We all went downstairs, and Daniel opened the kitchen door. There was my poor Troy in the cage foaming at the mouth. He was snarling at Daniel. "What did you do to him, he was fine with me?"

He was baring his teeth and snapping at Daniel. He had peed in the cage, and it was extraordinarily strong smelling. His back legs were very wobbly unlike they used to be. I opened the back door to try and get him outside. He struggled at first but then managed to drag himself outside, I also put a big bowl of water down for him.

"You haven't answered me! What did you do to him?"

Daniel said, "Nothing, just playing." Daniel phoned the vet, and he was told if there's no change by morning to take him down. The rest of the night, I prayed for my lovely dog to get better, but he was just getting worse.

The next morning, we took him to the vets, and he said, "I'm sorry, it looks like he has been kicked or hit his head, but he has distemper, and it would be kinder to let him go. If you try to keep him going, he will be in more pain."

I said sniffling, "But he's only 18 months old."

"I know," he said, "...it happens though."

The vet asked, "If I need you to come and hold him, will you?"

"Yes, of course," I said. We handed him over. The children were in tears and didn't quite understand. They hugged him and we left. Troy turned and watched us leave, which was the most distressing part. Daniel, meanwhile, was back in the house, you know he never really liked Troy.

The walk home was quiet with stifled sobs and disbelief that such a lovely, healthy dog could have to go like that. As we got in the house, Daniel said, "Well, did it go ok?"

I said, "Yes," with tears dribbling down my cheek. He looked surprised saying, "I thought he would go to a loving home."

In the morning, the phone rang. It was the vets calling to see if I wanted to go and pick up his collar. So, solemnly, I trudged to the vets on my own and went in and I was called to the side room. There on the table was just his collar in a clear bag. I said, "Did he go well or was he difficult?"

The vet said, "He was as good as gold, such a lovely boy, he put his head on my knee and then he fell asleep. No problem with him at all."

"Such a shame," I blubbed as he handed me his collar.

His smell was all over it. I said thank you and quickly left the vets and went outside for a good old cry. I went home and put the collar under my pillow as I was missing him so much. I remembered the last words the vet said to me, it's not normal for an Alsatian to have fits, something bad must have happened.

Chapter 11
Time for a Change

My lovely mum was starting to get on a bit, and she was diagnosed with dementia. They took her away into a care home at Mull Hall. This was a very hard time for me, first losing Troy and then seeing her leave her lovely home in Dornoch.

One day, I was just lying on my bed hugging Troy's collar and sobbing quietly, when Caitlyn came in and tried to console me. I was missing him like crazy and was still puzzled at what had happened. I asked Caitlyn, could she have any idea what happened to our lovely boy Troy for him to go like that? She looked at me with eyes brimming with tears and said, "Dad was playing with him in the kitchen and at first it was a bark, then he was getting kicked and dad had his steel toe capped boot on his head. I came downstairs and saw the door open. Then he booted him in the head."

I burst into tears. "That's not on, that's very cruel. If I had known that, I would have reported him. He killed my lovely boy, Troy."

That night, I was still seething from what Caitlyn had told me. But I knew I couldn't do anything. It was her word against his. I sat reading my Bible and prayed hard. I needed someone to love and care for me as I am, not to treat me as his slave and as a prostitute. I did that every night. Caitlyn came into the bedroom and said that she really didn't like her dad for the bad way he is treating us all. I said, I really need to talk to him to get a grip and stop treating us like his slaves.

George was going with a lovely girl Rachel; she was from Tain. She came over for the weekend and stayed in Caitlyn's room. We had a good weekend together. Daniel was gone for a few days, and I was glad of the peace. Rachel said something strange to me.

She said, "There's something evil in this house and I don't like it. I'm not sure what it is, but it's not nice, it could be a person."

I just laughed and said jokingly, "Yes, my husband." As Rachel left, she said, "Thank you for a good weekend and please keep everyone safe from this evil thing."

"I said I hope it shows itself," and she said, "It will when it's ready." I took her home and we hugged.

A few months later, Caitlyn took ill again, and doctors were, yet again, unsure of what was causing it. She was admitted to hospital with pains in her belly and feeling nauseous. They first said it was gastroenteritis, she remained in for a few days, but the pains were getting stronger. They started giving her injections of morphine, these became more regular, and the pain was gradually getting stronger. I was at home when in the morning, I got a call saying that Caitlyn had been transferred to the coronary unit in Raigmore. Not to be scared, but her heart rate is not going as it should and her blood pressure is high. The staff was told to keep an eye the vitals until it gets stable.

I called Daniel and was crying so much after getting the call. I told him about Caitlyn, and he said, "Remember the good days with her. What will be will be?" When I heard that on the phone, I hung up and cried my eyes out and was very angry with Daniel. I prayed hard for strength for Caitlyn to fight this and strength for me to deal with the situation. I couldn't sleep a wink that night. In the morning, I called the hospital for an update and was told there was good and bad news, and I was asked to come in and see her and see the doctor. So, I went with George and Rachel, but as usual Daniel didn't want to go in.

She looked so much better when we arrived and there were no heart issues anymore, great news. But then I was told that her bladder was not working the way it should be. She was scanned and there was still urine retention in the bladder, and it wasn't fully emptying. This is where the pain was coming from. But the bad news is that Caitlyn will have to be catheterised for the rest of her life. We're so very sorry to have to tell you this. We know that you might not want to believe this but it's true and any other NHS hospital will tell you the same thing. A medical person asked, "If there was any stress at home or school? As it was the stress that started this off, but we're not sure what else?"

Caitlyn was allowed to come home but, was catheterised before she came home. When we got home, all Daniel was doing was rubbing his head. Caitlyn was feeling better, and her belly wasn't as sore as before.

A few days later, Caitlyn was feeling much better. I noticed that her underwear for washing had blood in it. I asked her what was happening, "Are you tugging the catheter?"

"No, I'm not tugging it."

"So, why are you bleeding down there? You're bleeding through the tube too? Maybe, it's not the right one."

I mentioned it to Daniel, but he was not fussed. So, I took her back to see the doctor and Dr Kelly checked it and said to me and Caitlyn, "Are you pulling it?"

We both said, "No!"

"But something or someone is?"

We both said, "No way!"

Caitlyn said to him, "Why would I want to cause it to hurt?" Dr Kelly called in a couple of nurses and had it removed. "Now, we'll see how you get on without it."

Everything was going well with me and the kids, it was just not going so well with me and Daniel. We were on the verge of splitting up as we weren't living together as a normal married couple. I had already decided that I will not be a slave to him anymore.

Caitlyn said, "There must be a decent man out there for you."

I replied, "I can't see me being happy again."

But she said, "You will, you just need to get out there and look. Try 'Tagged,' and see if you can find new friends and who knows?"

So, I listened to her advice, God knows you need to be happy. You will find a man who will love you for who you are. I was still unsure, but thought why not? I will try it. I will give it a go, but if it's a weird site I am coming off.

So, I signed up for 'Tagged,' a dating and friendship website. It wasn't too bad; I found several friends and there were also several weirdoes. But I was chatting to several men on there. But there was only one who I really liked. That was Dave. He chatted to me, and we were just talking away, and it was a lovely different form of chatting than my husband Daniel. I got a fright though, as he said that he had seen me somewhere before. I was shocked and trying to rack my brains as to where he had seen me before? I mean, had he? When? I laughed nervously and Caitlyn said, "See, I notice you are laughing again, and you are happy." Yes, I am very. I still couldn't think where we had seen each other. I still felt more at ease when I was talking to him.

Caitlyn said, "I am glad, cos I am happy too and I'm with a nice guy called Steve." Steve even said to me that he will take care of Caitlyn and take her out most of the time. I was incredibly happy that he did that, as she needed to get out. As Daniel and I we were now separated, although still in the same house, he noticed Caitlyn was now happy and just said that Steve was a weird guy.

I said to my husband Daniel, you can stay here until you find somewhere else to live. He thanked me for that and agreed. Even though we were living separate lives, we were still arguing most of the time.

It was like I was treading on eggshells, and I couldn't do anything right. He said he was not happy with Caitlyn being with Steve, as he was not the right one for her. He didn't like him being with her. He even took Caitlyn aside when she came home, saying, "I do not like you being with him, he is not suitable for you. I don't like him."

She answered back, trying to be tough in front of him, "I don't care if you don't like him, and he is with me not you. We are going to be engaged and we are in love!"

He said, "You will not sleep with him, while I am living here!"

She yelled back, "You have no control over my life!"

Daniel was due on night shift, so Steve when he came over to see Caitlyn asked me if he could stay over with Caitlyn. He said he would leave first thing in the morning. I said if Caitlyn wants you to. I can see that you are both in love. I went online onto Tagged and continued chatting with my friends. Dave and I were exchanging phone numbers, so we could keep in touch with each other.

Daniel wanted a lift to work and as he went upstairs to change, he went into Caitlyn's room and said, "Don't be taking people into your room. Do you understand me?"

He was not happy about their relationship as he thought Steve was very weird, or so he said. As I drove him to work, he said, "Heather, keep her away from Steve, as I know they're getting engaged and supposedly in love, but don't let them sleep together."

I dropped him off and drove back and Steve was at the house with Caitlyn. He asked me again and I said if Caitlyn wants you to. "I promise, I'll be away before that evil man comes home," said Steve. I allowed it although, I was still nervous, and I made sure he had left before Daniel came home in the morning.

Caitlyn was saying to me, "Please don't tell him Steve was here."

I said, "Don't worry, I won't." I picked Daniel up from work.

He started again. "Caitlyn had better have been a good girl, or she has me to deal with."

I said to him, "Leave her alone, she is not a baby, and she has a boyfriend. She needs happiness, rather than you are moaning about it."

When we arrived at home, he went into the house and was sniffing quite loudly, so I said to him, "Have you got the cold?"

He said "No! I can smell a man's scent; a man has been in this house, and it had better not have been him!"

I said to him, "Daniel! You can stop this, or you can leave now."

So, he shut up. "I said nobody has been here." I felt ashamed for telling lies and prayed for forgiveness.

The next day, Daniel offered to make a special meal for us all, especially as it was his last few days living with us. He was going to be going for good. The meal smelt lovely when I came in from work. He served everyone else however Caitlyn's and my plates were separate from the others. Everyone was eating nice, and it tasted good at first. Then I started to feel queasy, and I said to him, "Is there something wrong with this food?"

Daniel said, "No! It's nice"

Tanya and George were also eating theirs. Caitlyn also started to feel queasy, and we both were going a wee bit pale and sickly.

Daniel said, "I don't know what's up with you two, it's lovely."

Caitlyn and I went into the kitchen and cleaned the plates into the bin. We went to bed that night and we had stomach pains all night and we were both sick all night. In the morning, everyone else was fine apart from the both of us. Daniel was very chirpy and smiling as he looked at us both. He whistled as he walked out the door to walk to work. We looked at each other and wondered, was it him?

Daniel came home and phoned a local hotel to stay for a night until his brother could pick him up to move back to Glasgow. I was so relieved that he was doing that, then I thought I might be able to relax. Steve came over to see Caitlyn and was raging and said he would go and have it out with Daniel. I thought he was going to punch him. They were both yelling at each other and then it went quiet, and I thought someone has got hurt. We went inside and Daniel was patting Steve on the shoulder. "We're best buddies now, aren't we, my boy?"

Steve smiled and said, "Yes."

I had put all his bags in the car and drove him to the hotel in Alness. I said to him I didn't ever want to see him back and never to get in touch with us again after the way he had treated us. He agreed and smiled as I dropped him off.

Steve was with Caitlyn when I returned, and they were sharing alternating weekends at his parents' house and mine until they got a place for them both to live together. I was still chatting to my friends online and I was so glad to have a nice man to chat to and Dave was my kind of guy. We hit it off almost at once.

The days went by, and I was still doing the commute to Inverness every day, 40 minutes each way and sometimes more in rush hour. I wanted a place closer to my work, so I went to my housing provider to see if there were any properties closer to my workplace. They said they would look for me and for Steve and Caitlyn as they needed a place too.

They had got a flat in Muir of Ord next to the distillery for a fresh start as they were now engaged. I went to visit my other daughter Tanya and her husband Jeremy; they were at his mum's house. I told them what had happened, and they said that I was well shot of him. I also mentioned that I have a nice man friend, but he is different from the others.

They said, "As long as he is a good person." I also mentioned that Caitlyn and Steve had a wonderful place to start their fresh life together in Muir of Ord. Jeremy and Tanya were happy for them especially after what Daniel had put them through.

A few days later, I received a phone call from the housing association to say that they had found a flat for me and would I like to view it? I said, "Yes, of course, I would." It would be great to have a fresh start and to get out of that house and its memories. I went to view the flat in Inverness with George.

We were happy to be in a fresh new building. The only problem I would have would be to downsize a four-bedroom house into a two-bedroom flat. Lots of stuff would have to go. This was the most upsetting part. I had spent quite a bit of money on the house over the years, but I was determined.

Caitlyn and Steve both helped me to pack everything, and she said, "I will be deeply sorry leaving here, but I am glad to be having a fresh start with my future husband to be. There are a lot of bad memories in this home."

I assumed she meant like the stabbing years ago and just nodded. She said, "But you are away from him now," and I said, "Thank God I am!"

We decided to get a new dog for the new home, and we called her Lucky. She is a lovely black dog who is very protective of me.

I was still chatting to Dave and the texts and phone calls were getting longer and more intense. We even sent pictures of each other although, I was very shy and only sent him ten-year-old photos, in case he didn't like how I looked. He said that he was thinking of coming up from Norfolk to meet me and I was a wee bit scared and excited. So, we set a date for that. I told him that I was in the middle of moving home, and he said that's fine, just let me know when you are settled, and I will arrange to come up to meet you. I was pleased he was so understanding.

As I was slowly getting settled, I said to Dave that he could consider a time to come up if he wanted to. He said that he would have to check hotels. I said that he could come up and stay at mine for the weekend. I don't know why I said that—he could have been an axe murderer for all we knew. But I felt calm and at peace, so I asked him to come up anyway. We arranged it for the first weekend in November 2015.

It was the last week in October, and I was getting extremely nervous. I told Caitlyn and Steve that he was coming up that weekend.

"That's great, let us know how you get on."

The day before he was due to come up, it was Wednesday afternoon and my belly was rumbling and churning like a cement mixer. Once more I spoke to the kids and said, "Am I doing the right thing?"

They said, "Yes, it's for your happiness." Dave was on the phone at 6 p.m. that night saying that he was driving through the night tomorrow to come and meet me and my family and stay until Sunday morning then go back down home again. George and I were nervous of meeting him.

The evening arrived and he was phoning me at almost every stage when he stopped for food and fuel. He phoned me about 3 a.m. and sounded a wee bit excitable. I asked him what was the matter? He said the road was very foggy and his fog lights weren't working but he would be there. As it approached 7 a.m., Dave phoned me again and said, "I'm coming into Inverness, I won't be long." I was pacing up and down the sitting room and my belly was going crazy. I looked out of the kitchen window and as he said he was turning in now, I knew it was his car. I started shaking and George came through and sat on the sofa. I heard the doorbell go on the intercom. I buzzed him in and heard footsteps on the stone steps leading up to the front door. My legs were weakening, and my belly was still going crazy, then the doorbell went, I said to George, "Please can you answer it?"

He said, "No! It's your man and your future."

So, I gathered up all my strength and gulped. I walked to the spy hole but couldn't see anyone. When I opened the door, my arms and legs and whole body was shaking. Here he was standing there before me. He said with a smile "I thought you weren't going to let me in." Lucky, my dog, got very excited and started to jump all over Dave, licking his hands and wagging her tail like a windmill. I shooed her away, and glanced at him, then went into full-on shy mode and looked down. I was very scared as he was a big guy.

He said to me, "No need to be shy, come here." He opened his big arms, and he gave me the longest hug ever. To my surprise, all the tension and stress disappeared. I felt so warm and loved even though it had only been for a few minutes. It was awesome. I introduced George and he shook his hand. George said he will leave the two of us together. We chatted for a while, and it felt like I had known him forever. All my nerves and anxiousness were gone. He said that he was very tired, and asked if could rest a while? I showed him through to my bedroom and left him to have a sleep. Caitlyn called me as I was just sat down for a ciggy and a coffee. She said, "Well? Did he arrive then?"

I said, "Yes, he is resting."

"Is he what you expected?"

"Yes, all I expected and more, I feel like I have known him forever. We will all go out for dinner tonight to a restaurant, so you can meet him then. He is only up here until Sunday."

She said, "That would be fine."

After about four hours, Dave came through and said, "Thank you for letting me rest. I needed that!"

Lucky jumped up on the couch and cuddled with Dave as soon as he sat down, licking his face.

I just blushed and carried on tidying up and offered him a coffee. Then we just sat and chatted for hours, and we cuddled up together on the sofa, with Lucky trying to sit in-between us. This felt so right, better than I had ever felt. I said that my daughter Caitlyn and her fiancé Steve were coming over tonight, and then we can go out for dinner. He said that would be nice. I just cuddled up to him and he was so cuddly, and I felt safe for the first time ever. Where the hours went, I couldn't say, we just were so happy cuddling up. That afternoon, Dave asked me where the Driver Hire place was, and I took him over there to see about work availability here. I was surprised. "I didn't know that was what you wanted?"

He said, "Its worth an ask, just in case we move forward with us."

I was so happy and felt so warm.

As we went back to the flat, we sat and just cuddled up and rested in each other's company. Then the doorbell went, and I went to press the access button and Caitlyn and Steve just came up the stairs and came in. Things were going well, and Dave hugged Caitlyn and shook Steve's hand. We were just chatting away and waiting for George to arrive home. As soon as he arrived, we got changed and went out for our meal. We had a very enjoyable time, but Caitlyn kept staring at Dave and he was staring back. I didn't know what to make of it.

We had a few drinks, and I was so happy to see us all getting on. After the meal, we left and went outside for a ciggy. Steve shook Dave's hand saying, "Nice meeting you, pal," and Caitlyn went in for a hug. "Nice meeting you. Can I call you dad?"

Dave looked surprised and said, "Of course, you can."

She smiled and skipped off with Steve. She shouted back, "Hope to see you soon."

Dave replied, "You will!" Steve drove off in his car and we waited for the taxi.

Caitlyn texted Dave and said, "Love you, dad. See you again soon, I hope. xx." This shocked us both.

The taxi came and took us back to the flat and Dave stayed with me in my bed, and it was wonderful. I felt loved again and couldn't believe that such a man existed. Dave said the same to me. We fell asleep in each other's arms.

The next day, we awoke mid-morning and we decided to take Dave to see the sights in Inverness. After all, he had told me he had only been here delivering goods to shops and never stayed. I showed him around the river, the castle, the canal and a lovely café in the market. We then returned home to relax as I knew Dave would need rest as tomorrow, he would have to return down south, but I won't say return 'home.' We sat and watched a movie and ordered a takeaway and Dave commented on how expensive the food was. I said, "It's reasonable for up here!"

We just laughed it off and enjoyed having cuddles and George just sat there and smiled and blushed too. He was happy to see me happy.

Early Sunday morning, we were awake at 7 a.m. and Dave was again packing his bags to return to England. The sky was very orange. It looked horrible. Not calm, and peaceful like I was. I didn't want him to go. His car raised my spirits as it didn't want to start! But eventually, it did. He reminded me of the fog coming up and he thought that someone upstairs must like him as the car felt like it was driving itself.

He said that he was a Christian and had prayed to God to help him get here safely and he did. So, prayer does work. The time came to say our goodbyes and he said to me, "I will be back."

But I thought it was a flash in the pan and it was just a dirty weekend to him. But we hugged and kissed, and Dave thanked me for the weekend, he repeated that he would be in touch, and he would be back again. We kissed and hugged once more. And he drove out of the car park as we waved him off.

I cried and cried, I honestly thought that was it and I would never see him again. George asked me why Dave had to go back? I said that he must go back to work on Monday.

We then got into the car and headed back to our old house in Fraser Road, Invergordon to clean up and clear the house, ready to hand the keys back on Monday morning. I asked George and Caitlyn and Steve "What do you all think of Dave?"

Steve said, "He is a nice man."

Caitlyn said, "I like him mum, he is the one for you."

I asked her, "How do you know that?"

She said, "I was talking to God, and he said it." I just shrugged my shoulders and just looked at her in disbelief.

It was 10 p.m. and Dave phoned me and said he was back home safe. The rain was teeming down in Glasgow, but he made it safely. He said that he was sorry to leave me, but he will be back. I said that would be great. That night, I prayed so hard to be allowed to see him again. I longed to hold him again and smelled his aftershave on the pillow. I also prayed that next time would be for a wee bit longer. I had never met such a gentle giant as he.

In the morning, I was hard at work in the old house in Invergordon with Steve and Caitlyn. We were just sitting down for a ciggy and a coffee break when I received a call from Dave. I was so incredibly happy to be receiving a call from my lovely man.

He said, "Hi, darling. How are you doing?"

I said, "Fine."

He said, "Do you want some good news?"

So, I said, "What is the good news?"

He said, "Are you sitting down?"

I said, "Yes, why?"

He said that he was handing his notice in tomorrow and he would be moving up to be with me in four weeks' time! Not for a day, or a weekend, or a week, but, for good! How's that for good news? I was so shocked; I gasped and dropped my coffee on the floor.

I shouted, "Really?"

Dave replied "Yes!"

"Oh my goodness!" I was so shocked; I could hardly speak. Caitlyn and Steve heard my yelp and loud shout.

"What is it? What's up Mum?"

"Dave's coming up for good!"

"Whoopie!"

She was over the moon. To me, I thought it was a dream. I was overjoyed with him moving up in four weeks. So, as it was getting closer to December, I had to get everything sorted in the house and at work. I prayed that night and thanked God for bringing my Dave back to me. Now, I have something to focus on at work and at home. I was surprised at the short notice, but this love of mine was already very deep and growing fast. I had Steve, Caitlyn and George to help me get settled in before my Dave moves up to be with me for good!

Chapter 12
In Sickness and in Health

Dave was on his journey coming back up to Inverness, to his new home with me! I was so excited. I couldn't wait for the love of my life coming back to me. I couldn't sleep with excitement, and I was praying for him to arrive here in Inverness safely. It came to an hour before Dave was arriving at the flat. I had the cups ready for when he arrived in the flat, and I was ready to make him a well-earned cup of coffee. Steve, Caitlyn, and George were going to be here too to welcome him into the flat. The door buzzer went, and I ran down the stairs to see him, and I just kissed him and hugged him tight. He had six black plastic bin bags and his big family Bible. I thought to myself, The Bible says it all: He must be a Christian and a good man. We had coffee together after he had taken his rental car back. We began to relax, and he felt relieved. I said, "I am so happy you are here with me!" He said the same to me.

That evening, we all went out for a meal, rather than having to cook. We were all having an enjoyable time, and everyone was relaxed. No more having to drive up and down the country, my life was finally falling into place. My prayers were being answered. Dave said that he would find a job, and everything would be fine now we're together.

Steve and Caitlyn were longing to get married, but Steve's parents were saying to wait longer as it's only a year since they were engaged. As we finished our meal and drinks, we all decided we should leave for our homes. Dave was polite but was yawning as he was very tired from his long drive the night before. Steve and Caitlyn went to their flat in Muir of Ord and we went home to our flat.

Our first night together was so relaxed and as we climbed into bed, we chatted for hours and cuddled, and wished each other, "Good night and God bless you." How wonderful it was to wake up next to my man Dave. He was so big and strong, and I just watched him sleep. He opened his eyes and we both smiled at each other. Good morning, we shared. I got up and got us both a coffee and a ciggy. We were both chatting while still in bed. He said to me, "Are you a Christian?"

I said "Yes, why?"

He said, "If I find us a nice church, will you go with me?"

I said, "Of course, I will."

I knew that I would have to work next Sunday shift at the care home. But this week, Dave's first week with us, he was going to be looking for work. He signed up for Driver Hire and waited to be called. The week passed by quickly and everything was going really well. I never thought I would be this happy.

Sunday, I went to work, and Dave set off to find a church for us. I finished my shift and Dave had made us a lovely dinner; I was being spoiled. He said that he had found a lovely church for us. It was Inverness Baptist Church; it was next to the castle. He said the people were so lovely to him and so welcoming. There was an old lady called Janet, who just came up and introduced herself and gave him a huge hug. The pastor came over and introduced himself and shook his hand. Wow! That's fantastic! And the church has a live band too.

The next Sunday, I was off, and we went. But, as I was getting nearer to the door, I felt a voice saying to me, "You don't need to go into there. You don't need this."

But Dave, said to me, "Don't be afraid."

So, I went in, and Janet ran up to me, hugged us both, and said welcome back. Iain, the pastor, came over too. The band was particularly good, and I said how different it was from the 'Free Church' I had attended years ago. I was amazed and so happy that this was the church to which we both belonged. Life was finally going right! How had it taken so long to find a decent man and a great church? Our God is good.

We went home and had a wonderful roast dinner and George was incredibly happy at having it. Dave had proved himself to be good cook and we were well fed. I called Caitlyn and told her that we had been to church, and it was a fantastic church full of lovely people and said that she should come along too. She said that she didn't know if it was her thing or Steve's. But I said you don't know what you're missing. The next Sunday, we all, Steve, Caitlyn, Dave and I, went to church, and George was working. We all enjoyed ourselves and after the service, we were invited in for tea and coffee and cake. Julie, the pastor's wife, Janet and Harold, Janet's husband, were so welcoming. We left saying that we would be back, unless I was working, and I would send Dave in my car. Steve said, "If Mam's working, I could drive you." We all went back to the flat and Dave had again cooked us a lovely dinner, all homemade. I couldn't believe it. What had I done right? After dinner, we went to the river and had a walk and played with Lucky. I showed Dave more nice places to visit, and he said, "I am home."

I said, "Do you love it here?"

He said, "Yes, I do. I used to deliver here in my lorry to the retail park."

We sat down on the bench and chatted about our future plans. It felt right, much better than my last three husbands. They were just not talkers, caring or considerate. I also told Dave that I find the river soothing, it lets your problems float away with the water. We had to be honest with each other and shared our tales about our lives before and Dave told me about his ex-wife June, who he had married for just a month! I was a wee bit shocked but understood as he continued and said that he had been married three times and his first wife Lisa, had a mental illness, and committed suicide in 2006, leaving him with their three children to bring up. So terribly sad and also, his second ex-wife Lorraine committed adultery on him. I didn't like cheaters. The last wife, June was told about the other two wives, and she promised Dave that she wouldn't be like the others, but just after they came back from their honeymoon, she attempted suicide. Dave had a wee breakdown and couldn't stay with her after she had promised that she wouldn't. I guess that's kind of understandable. But I couldn't bring myself to tell him my little secret, just yet.

I decided to introduce Dave to my mum, who was in Mull Hall care home at the time. Dave bought flowers for her, which surprised her, and she looked at him like he had three heads! We had a nice time seeing her, but it wasn't long before we had to leave. Time had flown, seeing my lovely mum in this place was harder than I thought it would be.

I went back to work on the Monday away with the car, while Dave went to Driver Hire to sign up for them.

That night, when I returned home, Dave suggested that he be put on the insurance for the car and use the car during the day and drop me into work and pick me up every day. Also, it meant it was easier going to church. I wasn't allowed the weekend off, so I missed it, but the kids went. They all had a great time despite me not being there. After a week had passed, I had a fall out with my boss, she was so horrible to me, I was being taken advantage of all the time, she wasn't very friendly with Dave either, so I decided to hand in my notice and find another job. I had had enough!

Caitlyn and Steve got married in the spring of 2017, at the Baptist Church, and Dave's son James came up for the wedding, meeting us all for the first time in person. He even wore a kilt to the wedding, which was a good laugh!

Dave got part-time temporary jobs with different truck companies, but they were taking advantage of him too. We both thought of looking elsewhere, until a job came up at a nursing home in Daviot called Meallmore. I previously worked as a care assistant and loved the job. Caitlyn and Steve unfortunately split up due to severe marriage difficulties and suspicions of assault. She found her own flat by herself and George moved out too into his own place. He didn't like staying with his mum and stepdad. He wanted to live his own life.

I decided to have a few drinks in the flat as I knew I had to get my secret out to Dave. He had been honest with me about his most recent marriage and separation. Now, it was my turn. We both sat down, and I began. I was a wee bit 'tiddly,' but I went into telling Dave about Daniel. I had mentioned that I was single on Tagged and I had to set the record straight. I had felt like I had been separated for far longer as we had separate bedrooms. He was lovely about it and said, it makes no difference, he was still deeply in love with me. I was ashamed that I needed some drinks before telling him. I thought that it was worse than murder. But Dave calmed me down and was so accepting of it.

I was invited for the interview for Meallmore, and I was offered the job, which I loved doing. They knew my back was not great, but with care and support, I would manage. I had to refresh my moving and handling training, which I did. It was great, no problems. Dave was pleased for me and took me to work every night and then said that he would like to take me and the family out for dinner. So, we arranged for the next day I was off to go out to Jimmy Chungs, our favourite Chinese buffet restaurant.

I didn't know the kids were going to be there before us, but when we arrived, they were all sat at the table, waiting patiently for word on why Dave had called them all there. We all ate and had a good time, then something, I hadn't expected happened. Dave stood up and went down on one knee to propose to me. He said, "Will you be my wife? I know we've not been together that long but, I feel like I have known you forever and I want you to be mine." I was so delighted and smiled and said yes. We had lots of drinks and returned home happy with a lovely ring on my finger. I thought I was dreaming, but it was all true. I had the weekend off, so we spent it with family. I was made a lovely tea by my lovely fiancé. I was so very happy.

I was next on night shift, and I enjoyed my job. I was sent onto the second floor, which is a heavy floor. I didn't like it, but I carried on doing what I was told. The team I was placed with were all Polish. They all went out to have a smoke break, which was wrong of them, and I was left all on my own on the floor. Anything could have happened. I heard a cry from a room, and I hurried down the corridor to where I heard the cry. There was a poorly elderly gentleman on the floor. He had fallen from his bed and was lying in his own urine and faecal matter. I went to search for help, but nobody was there, and I pushed the emergency button, but still no help. I called down the stairs to the fire exit where they were all smoking and they said they would be there in a few minutes, just leave him. But, in my own mind and heart, I just couldn't leave him like that. I just couldn't. So, I decided to help him on my own and with his aid, we managed to get him on his chair. I managed to clean him up and change his bed. He smiled weakly and said, "Thank you." I felt a hard click in my spine and I felt sick. I heard the others coming back in now. "Oh, you've done him, he could have waited." I disagreed. I went to see the nurse on duty and told her what had happened, and she was furious. "They shouldn't have left you on your own on the floor, especially with your back!" I couldn't cope with the pain, and I had to ask the nurse to call Dave to take me home at 3 a.m.

The staff nurse said, "I hope you're feeling better for tomorrow." When Dave arrived to pick me up, I told him what had happened, and he said I just needed to rest until tomorrow night, and then see how I was. He managed to help me get undressed and into bed. So, I rested until about 5 p.m. and it was time to get up. Dave went through to make me a coffee before dinner. I reached over to open the blind and my back clicked again, and I was paralysed. I couldn't move and the pain was intense. I couldn't feel my feet or legs. I asked Dave to get a pen to see if I could feel my feet. Nothing, Dave said he was going to call the ambulance, but I was trying to be stubborn, but the pain was too much for me.

He called the ambulance, and they were very uncertain as to what had happened, but they managed to get me in the ambulance to the hospital. I had X rays, an MRI scan and was in front of the surgeons. They were quite worried in case the paralysis was going to be permanent. After the check-up, I was sent home with heavy painkillers, and they called for me in an outpatient's appointment and I was diagnosed with Disc Deteriorating Disease, which I was told could be age related and if it got much worse and I was immobile, they would freeze my spine and I would be in a wheelchair for life. I was sent to the physiotherapists and into the warm puffin pool, but I couldn't feel the floor. They gave me walking aids, which I hate with a passion!

It was awful having to cope with walking aids, I was so stubborn and wouldn't accept what I had been told. I wanted to throw my sticks in the canal and said this so many times to Dave and he jokingly said that he would throw me in to get them. Cheek! I just had to bear with it as it was helping me, even though I didn't want to admit it. James, Dave's eldest son was coming up from Nottingham regularly to see us now and he was just like the medical staff, both he and Caitlyn were forever pushing me to use my walking aids. It felt like I couldn't win, it was like murder. We started going to church every Sunday. We were offered a ground-floor flat without stairs and a disabled wet room for a bathroom. There was a lovely view from the back garden. We were given four days' notice to move into it. It was all systems go using George's battered old first car, taking all the boxes and other bits, while we hired a man with a van to take the rest of the furniture. Caitlyn was now living in our old flat with her friend Rachel.

We were going on a weeks' holiday to see Dave's family in England. We were offered a pet sitter to look after our dog Lucky. The offer came from our neighbours across the road. They said, "We will look after your dog while you are away for a week, don't worry."

We were delighted and left them with the house keys to get more stuff if Lucky needed it. We had an enjoyable time with Dave's family. On returning home, we were looking forward to seeing Lucky and we had bought a present for the neighbours as a thank you for looking after her.

However, when we returned home, Carter brought out the dog and handed me the keys and we said, "How was she?" He said everything was fine. We gave them the present and he rushed inside. We also went to see our next-door neighbours with their present and they were saying that while we were away, Carter and his wife Teresa and their next-door neighbour were going in and out of our flat and they think we may have been robbed. I said that when we came in the fridge door was open and food was missing. Yes, that would be it. Also, I checked my jewellery box and there was quite a bit missing especially what Dave had bought me. But we had no proof, so we had to leave it and we had the locks changed. Nowadays, they can't even look us in the face as they're wracked with guilt.

As Father's Day approached, we got a call from Mull Hall care home who said we should visit my mum as she had taken a turn for the worst. She was not eating and had lost a great deal of weight and the doctor had said she is near death. Dave and I decided to sit with mum over night for three nights and she was barely breathing or speaking. This was a very difficult time for me. Dave was my rock. I just couldn't face being here on my own and he was just wanting to be there for me and my mum.

Throughout the nights, we were both taking it in turns to go out for a ciggy and Dave was speaking to mum when I returned, and he said that he had promised her that he would always love me. He said mum let out a wee murmur as he said that. She must have heard him. Then Dave went out for a ciggy, and I stood next to mum and whispered to her, "I've told him, so there are no more secrets." Mum murmured and a weak smile appeared on her face. As a nurse, I always remembered that the hearing was the last sense to go. She must have heard everything. Then when Dave came back in, I told him what I had just told mum.

The three nights went very slowly, and it was a very painful experience to watch my mum suffer, after she had done everything for me and supported me through my heart surgery and all my other bad times. She was the only parent I had ever known and here she was, a frail old lady, rasping and trying to breathe, her bright blue eyes sparkling, waiting for the call from her Lord. The final morning came, and we were told to prepare the family for mum's death. The whole family turned up at mum's bedside, but Jonas was not there as he had to work and wasn't given enough notice to get time off from the Oil Rig. The whole room was very sombre and Jemma, my niece, wet my mum's mouth with a swab. Her mum, my sister-in-law told her to leave her alone. But Jemma argued back. "She's my granny and I will give her mouth a clean."

Her mum sat back down, clearly still annoyed. We were there for about four hours and Leslie; Jonas' wife phoned him, and the sobs could be heard down the phone. Here was a man who so loved his mum and couldn't be there at this sad time. The shaky voice was saying just how much he loved his mum, and you could hear the sorrow in his voice.

Then came the time for mum to breathe her last and Jonas could be heard crying aloud over the phone, the kids were all crying, and I was holding her hand until it just dropped, and I knew that she had gone to be with her Lord Jesus.

This was one of the hardest things I have ever experienced. Dave had already lost both his parents and he was comforting everyone. Apart from Leslie who just picked stuff up and wanted to leave with it wrapped in a shawl. Dave said that he knew mum had gone as he saw something pass him. I was so grateful that Dave was there for this and for me. I don't know what I would have done if I wasn't with Dave. He actually supported me; unlike some people I'd rather forget. The date was 9 June 2016, Father's Day. I will never forget that date. She was the matriarch and my confidant. But most of all she was my lovely mum, and a wonderful granny and very great great-granny to all her little ones.

The funeral was on the following Friday, this was even more poignant, this was her birthday. Dave and the family carried the coffin over to the graveside and placed it on the planks over the grave. As it was the last plot in the family grave, it wasn't too deep. I had to hold a cord and Jonas another. He was very gaunt and pallid, and it showed just how much he loved his mum. Jonas and I were the last two to let go of the cord. Dave did something rather unexpected. Everyone was shocked. Dave brought out a large bottle of whisky and offered a dram to everyone there. As my mum was a whisky drinker, he thought this was fitting. Everyone drank in a wee toast and left for the wake. Dave, however poured some whisky on the coffin and gave mum a lovely send off. I couldn't believe it, an Englishman, toasting a highlander with Scotch and everyone approved. Wow! I think mum would have told him it was a waste though.

The wake went well, and we had soup and sandwiches, and Jonas and Dave bought each other whisky. Jonas thanked Dave for all that he did to help. They parted as friends.

A few months later, I heard in the church about believers' baptism and wondered what it was. I spoke to Dave and Ian, the pastor and they explained that it's a public declaration of your love for Jesus. "You go into the baptismal pool and go under the water and symbolically, you are buried with Jesus as he was buried. Then you are raised from the water as Jesus was raised to a new life, just as you are raised into a clean and living way."

"So, what's special about the water?" I said.

"Nothing," said Ian, "it's just normal water." So, I decided that I would want to be baptised and had to meet with Iain for a couple of times to talk through the baptismal procedure.

Then the actual Sunday arrived, I was quite nervous and had both walking aids. First, Brock was baptised, and it was amazing. Then it was my turn. I walk over to the microphone and gave my testimony and added that no matter the pain I am in just now, Our Lord and Saviour suffered far more pain than I. There were several sobs and calls of Amen. I was helped into the pool by Dave and Ian and Gordon. Being baptised that day was awesome, like I had died with Jesus and raised again to new life. As I got out of the pool, it felt strange. I had absolutely no pain whatsoever. Janet tried to help me, but I said I have no pain. She exclaimed, "Praise the Lord."

Everyone was amazed as we shared tea and coffee and cakes. I even turned to Dave and asked him when I came up and just before I went down under, who was holding my back? Dave said that nobody was anywhere near me. To which, I said that I had a hand touching my back and when I was under the water, it was a hand with a white sleeve like a robe, helping me up.

Dave said, "Wow! That's special. Jesus must have been holding you and because of what you said before you were baptised, maybe Jesus gave you the period of no pain."

I was overjoyed, thinking that I would be able to go back to work. I told Dave this and he said, "Let's just see how you are tomorrow."

When we arrived home, I was still buzzing and doing everything. The kids had all gone home and at exactly 7 p.m., the pain returned with a vengeance. I was upset and cried on Dave's shoulder. "Ah well, he said, at least you had seven hours pain free. Most people don't even get that." But I did feel a wee bit different, I could feel God's presence in my heart and soul. I felt happier, and it was just like walking on air. If it wasn't for the pain, I would be fantastic.

Caitlyn had a bad accident in the old flat and cracked her head on the taps after she suffered a seizure. Rachel phoned us and we went over, and Caitlyn refused an ambulance, so we took her to A&E at Raigmore Hospital, they just said it's possibly just concussion. As nobody was doing anything, Dave was asking for a second opinion. They said they would but then they just discharged her. So, Dave took us to Aberdeen Hospital, and she was seen by a neurophysiological professor. She was having some non-epileptic seizures and he said it looked like Hoover's Sign. The professor helped Caitlyn to understand it and then we all headed back home.

Rachel decided that she was going to get her own accommodation, which she did, and she was given a bungalow in Alness. Caitlyn, as she was under special needs, she came to stay with us.

Caitlyn's social worker asked that Caitlyn be placed under guardianship, as she lacked capacity in so many areas. She also suffered PTSD, but at the time, nobody knew why? She was with us for almost a year when her guardian had arranged for Caitlyn to be moved into a supported living complex. She was happy when she first arrived as she made lots of new friends. She was coming on in leaps and bounds. It later transpired that Caitlyn's father had been abusing her for years, but the courts could do nothing as it was just her word against his. So, this was why Caitlyn had and was suffering so much.

We, Dave, and I, had arranged a date for our wedding. This was to be 22 June 2019. We had found a venue and we planned to use the Baptist Church for the ceremony. The venue was the Jury's Inn. We could only afford 50 guests and the planning was ongoing and as we were both on benefits and needed to save almost £3000. It was extremely hard going. I was always moaning to Dave that why couldn't we go anywhere or spend on takeaways? Dave simply reminded me that if we want to get married, we will have to tighten our belts. I often snapped at him, saying do I really want to marry you anyway? But I always apologised, and we were fine again. I was hunting all over Inverness for a wedding dress. Everywhere I went to was, 'no, you're too big, you need to go online,' then I went to a specialist shop in Inverness. She looked me up and down and said, "I have got just the thing for you."

I was amazed that it fit me like a glove. I was so happy. It still fits me today. I was shocked as Dave had told me that there would be somewhere that the lady would just have one in your size. This was the week before I went for it. The men got their kilts and outfits and the bridesmaids. It all went smoothly, even though I was panicking inside. Dave took care of the bridesmaids' dresses, and they were lovely.

On the wedding day, Caitlyn was giving me away and we opened a bottle of wine, but I couldn't drink any of it. The bridesmaids were nearly all ready, Jemma was the maid of honour, and we were just waiting for Tanya, who was running late. Dave had organised a horse and carriage. It was wonderful. The horse had a mane plaited with ribbons. Caitlyn had her new boyfriend Kieran going with her to our wedding. The weather forecast was rainy, but the sun shone, and my dress glittered in the sunshine. It was like a fairy tale wedding. I walked into the church and couldn't speak as I hadn't had a drink so Iain the pastor offered me water. My heart skipped a beat as I walked down the aisle and tears tripped my face as I saw the empty chairs at the front with white roses on them, in memory of our absent parents. There was Dave and everything felt completely different from the other weddings I had been through. This felt real and true. The vows were based on the ancient Gaelic and although they were tricky, we managed them. We shared Holy Communion as a married couple, most of our non-Christian friends were puzzled, but Iain told them this was to put Jesus first in our relationship. Then we had a piper playing Amazing Grace inside the church. Wow! Goosebumps or what? Such a special day and forever in our hearts and memories.

The following Saturday, we went to Nottingham for a wedding blessing primarily for Dave's family who couldn't get to Scotland. We had a wonderful day there too, scorching hot weather and the bluest sky. Our Honeymoon was a week in Skegness first, then a week in Blackpool. We enjoyed fabulous weather and fantastic company, and we went to church both Sundays.

We were back for a wee while and I suffered a stroke, while watching Silent Witness on TV. I heard a voice calling to me, while I was deep in a trance. It said, "Heather, follow me." I slowly came out of the trance and Dave had phoned an ambulance who verified that I had a stroke. I was rushed to hospital, where they gave me scans and they found out I had partial brain damage on the right-hand side. I was sent to see a stroke specialist who put me on medication to calm it down. I have had several incidences after this, and as you can tell I am a survivor and incredibly lucky to have survived.

Caitlyn and Kieran got engaged and we all had a family celebration. They both had to save hard for their wedding. They found this exceedingly difficult, but Dave was their financial appointee and he saved it for them. Caitlyn had decided to be baptised and was one of three candidates who were baptised in the River Ness, and we joked that she would catch a fish. Kieran was so excited and was thrilled to see his wife having a bath, in his words.

Following this Kieran and George started coming regularly to church and everyone was so welcoming to them. A few months later, I had another minor stroke and was admitted to hospital. I had no feeling in my feet and as I was walking, I noticed my toes were blue. I was informed by a nurse that I had broken my toes. But there is nothing they can do except wait for it to heal. So many things were happening to me, and Dave was just so calm. Dave's son James moved up to stay with us, as he had just left a serious relationship. This was just before a deadly new virus was discovered. We were locked down for months. We had a few big arguments, but we understood each other afterwards. Not long after, my son George had to move from his bedsit as two people in the upstairs flat had been murdered while he was there, and it was recommended that he move out of there. So, Kieran gave up his old flat for George and went to live with Caitlyn, his fiancée.

As the months went on, Dave had managed to pay for everything for their wedding and he picked the dresses, both bridesmaids and bride. He arranged for the horse and carriage again. Everything was going to plan. The church was booked, the Chieftain Hotel, and all the food. Dave's family mostly came up from England this time.

The day of the wedding arrived, and it was a wet day, but after the vows and the service, the sun came out. We had lots of pictures and Caitlyn was so delighted with her new husband Kieran. We went to the Chieftain Hotel for the reception and dance. A good night was enjoyed by all.

The next week was time for their honeymoon, and as they were both under special needs, Dave and I had to be chaperones and go with them. We took them to Chapel St Leonards in Lincolnshire in Dave's sister's caravan. It was great at first, until about Tuesday, when Caitlyn's bladder stopped working and she went into urinary retention. She was passing blood through her urine, and she was extremely ill.

Dave took her to the nearest main A&E in Pilgrim's Hospital, Boston. Kieran and I waited outside in the car. Dave and Caitlyn were in there for seven hours and Caitlyn had to be catheterised, although she hated it. But they had told her she was incredibly lucky to be alive. If she had waited as she had wanted to, she could have died. I gave thanks to God for saving her and giving Dave the mind to take her to the hospital.

Dave and I have been married for several years now and the family unit is strong. We live in a small flat in Inverness waiting for something more practical that can deal with the electric wheelchair I now use. I call her Betsy, and I don't like her at all. Caitlyn and Kieran have set up in a lovely bungalow and are enjoying married life. James is now in his own flat, near the town centre. George is working and stable, in fact we all are stable and in a good place. I love seeing Dave play the drums in the church and take on the responsibilities of church leadership. James plays music for the church too, I'm so proud of him. I continue to deal with my several medical conditions but have found comfort in my faith.

I am not going to get all soppy with you, I simply wanted to tell my story.

So, I now see that I have been saved throughout my life for something. I don't yet know what. But I hope that my story has helped you see in some way. So, you see that no matter how many bad things happen in your life, you can still be happy in the end. Because, as my mum used to say, *everything happens for a reason.*

God Bless You All.

Afterword by Dave

Dear friends and all who have read this biography of my wife, Heather. I hope it helped you as it helped me while writing this. You may be asking, what pulls all this together?

Well, in listening to my wife as she dictated the story of her life, it became clear to me that there was a recurring pattern to her life. As from the attempted rape at aged fourteen, someone stopped the offender, the drowning incident, a man was there to save Heather. Heather's heart problems and deliverance from death by the eminent heart surgeon Sir Terrence English. Even the deliverance from being aboard the Herald of Free Enterprise as she had applied to work on it. The deliverance from all three violent ex-husbands and being saved from rape by a miraculous taxi driver appearing at just the right time, Coincidences. I hear you say. I believe not. I personally believe these were all angels sent to save Heather from these horrendous incidents. If the offender from Wick hadn't been disturbed things could have gone from bad to worse. The off-duty police officer who rescued Heather from the North Sea, especially as she had already drowned, and he was pumping her chest to bring her back to life. He also had to administer the kiss of life. As the heart surgeon said, Heather had a few days to live. Had she just done as the Scottish doctors in Raigmore had said, she would have been dead long ago, even her experiences with her three ex-husbands.

These were filled with violence, either drink fuelled or just psychotic tendencies. This is totally unacceptable. What happened to her human rights or her right to live in peace and safety?

When we get married, we think everything will be fine. Even when we marry in church, not everyone sticks to their vows, with beatings galore, cheating and stabbings. Heather was used by these men. She didn't deserve any of this. Yes, I understand she must share her part in this, but the men too instead of brushing it under the carpet must accept their violent part of this distressed life.

Heather has also been under severe stress and distress, with several happenings throughout her life. She deserves plaudits and praise for her extreme motherly love for her son George in helping him to walk and talk and be able to live a virtually normal life, instead of allowing him to be murdered by his father or even thrown into a care home. Such a caring woman should never have to suffer punishment as she did. Also, with her daughter Caitlyn and her own peculiar disabilities like George, but thankfully not the same. These two children have severe learning difficulties and have been successfully brought up as a testament to a wonderful caring mother, without the backing of a caring husband or partner. She is to be honoured for doing all of this for three children.

Heather's story is like her own dearly departed Mother Katie. She was left, in numerous ways by her partners. But she managed to bring up her two children in a successful way, to have the support she had in her later years. Katie was a

God-fearing lady and a true believer, who now rests with her Lord and Saviour.

Heather herself, would tell you, throughout her life, she has known of Jesus and God, but never fully believed in him. Although, since birth, it's quite clear to me, after hearing Heather's story, that God has been active in her life. She has been rescued, saved, and helped through several difficult situations and come out the other side a better person.

You might be reading this thinking, 'but nothing bad has happened to me or I can't remember.' I tell you that if you look back on your life, as I have, there will be incidents which have happened that can't be explained. Things that happened if one thing or another thing hadn't happened, I would have been in trouble. I know I have.

Have you?

Heather Ann Ducker, Let Me Get There Safely!

The trials of life come to Heather Ann from the beginnings of life but through all, she finds a drawing to her of the maker she so needs.

'A heart-warming, tale of true-life struggles and conquering all that comes her way by trusting…'

'Protection comes in different forms for the Highland lass…and I now believe in angels.'

A tale of a Highland girl, who finds protection from the least of places and endures all manner of things. Written from her own standpoint, Heather shares all to show people her maker and his love for her.

Thank you…